WHERE YOU LINGER AND OTHER STORIES

WHERE YOU LINGER AND OTHER STORIES

BONNIE JO
STUFFLEBEAM

WHERE YOU LINGER
AND OTHER STORIES

FOR MY SISTER

CONTENTS

FUBAR

FUBAR

WE'RE ABOUT TO GO CAMPING. Cathryn's undressing before the closet in her garage apartment. I'm trying not to watch, though she wants me to. Instead, I peer into her glass terrarium where the skeletons live, three of them: a dwarf T-Rex and two dwarf stegosauruses. The T-Rex stands atop a lonely pile of rocks.

"Who's going to watch the skeletons?" I ask.

"I was going to leave them extra food." Cathryn rummages through the clothes pile on the floor, such beautiful chaos. "You think that's okay?" I stare at her reflection in the glass. Her bra, lacey and black, makes me want to glimpse what's underneath, even though I have before, five times.

"I guess so," I say. I look back at the T-Rex. His name, Cathryn tells me, is Ronald. The steggos are called Thelma and Louise; she thinks she's being ironic. The T-Rex's bones are so small I'm sure that if I picked him up I would break him. His eyes are tiny as sequins and suspended in empty sockets. He wails like a cat in heat. "I think something's wrong," I say.

"He's just hungry, Emma. Feed him. Food's next to the cage."

I open the yellow bottle of skeleton food; the musty smell makes me cough. The bottle is full of squiggling little worms. I pour some into the terrarium. Ronald clambers down the rocks. He dips his jaw into the worm pile and scoops them into his mouth, swallows. I can see them travel down his throat and into his empty bone stomach where they wriggle inside him.

Cathryn clears her throat. She stands before me with her hands on her hips, wearing tight blue jeans and a bumblebee-striped halter top. She's dressed for clubbing, not camping, and I realize that the kind of camping we'll be doing won't require the hiking shoes or the toilet paper I brought. I tell her she looks great. She does. I look back at the tank. The T-Rex peers up at me.

"Let me free," he whispers. His voice is like an echo. I can't. We're going camping.

IN THE SHALLOW FOREST WE set up our tent. The land has been cleared for people, like us, who want to be in nature but not too far in. Our tent is a miniature house. The box says it will fit twenty people, but we've only got five. It has French doors that fold down and collapsible walls to give everyone a sense of privacy, but through the first night I hear Cathryn and Anne, the girlfriend she brought along, their heavy breath and little moans. They make the whole tent sweat.

The site is close to the river, but not too close. At night we cannot hear the current. The bathroom is just around the corner, and there's a leaky water faucet next to where we parked the car, ten feet from the tent. Our friend Wendi brought a portable mini fridge and a fan; they run on batteries, but the fridge eats two an hour, so we have to run to the store once a day and buy at least twelve packages of four. We make a game of it. In some ways the drive is the best part of the trip, mostly because Cathryn is the one with the car, and she's asked me to go with her each time. We roll the windows down. She talks about the new girl, Anne, how they've just met but already spend nearly every night together. Every word she says feels like a secret between us. I don't want to hear about Anne, but I don't not want to hear about her either, because I want to know if she's better than me. I want to know when we'll share a bed again. I try to deduce the information from the cutesy story of how they met at the campus coffee shop, but I can't, because Cathryn has always been unpredictable, mysterious. With her unflinching face, she reveals nothing. Every time she asks me to get in the car with her, I do.

The nearest trash can is two whole miles from our site, so we're forced to rough it in that regard at least, dumping our food scraps into a plastic bag. Most of what we brought is food. Peanut butter, bread, baked beans in a can and hot dogs with mustard, two bottles of cheap red wine and a plastic handle of rum. Our broke friend, Mike, does the cooking. It's his way of paying us back. He also does the majority of the drinking. He's brought his set of oils, and his paint-stained hands dye whatever he touches. Each hot dog bun has a blue handprint, and by the time dinner's finished, the rum bottle is covered in fingerprints.

The second night Wendi builds a fire; we sit around the flames. The smoke follows Cathryn. No matter where she sits, the wind moves in her direction. Finally, she settles in one spot, lights a cigarette, and lets the smoke clog her eyes. We play a drinking game, *Never Have I Ever*.

"Never have I ever been to Disneyworld," I say. Cathryn and Wendi put down a finger; they went there once together.

"Never have I ever done acid," Wendi says. The rest of us admit defeat.

"Never have I ever been in love," Cathryn says. No one puts down a finger; no one is sure enough to commit to that. We all four of us look at Cathryn through the smoke. Her hair is up. The skin of her neck glistens with sweat. That we all want her is common knowledge; we can't help ourselves. This is what holds our friendships together, the flame to which we are helpless as moths.

That night, as we sleep, trees rustle, and the fallen branches on the ground crack like knuckles. When I leave the tent early in the morning to walk to the restroom, I find the contents of our trash bag scattered, the bottom ripped. By the river I spot a leopard, its white fur stretched so tight the bones poke through. In the disappearing moonlight, I nearly see the heart pumping in its chest. It's looking right at me, and I stand and stare until the sun creeps up and the leopard, its fur no longer see-through, bounds into the brush.

Back at the campsite a crowd is gathered around the dying embers of last night's fire. A dodo skeleton hops around the fire pit. One of the bones from its foot is missing. Without the feathers it looks just like any other bird. We only know it's a dodo from its fat chest, and its dodo beak. Plus, it tells us what it is when we ask it.

Cathryn shoos the bird. "Go, fly away."

"Dodos don't fly," it says, lifting a bone wing. The invisible joints crack. "I'm stuck."

It hangs around until we change into our swimsuits and leave for the swimming hole. It's only a couple of miles away, so we walk. Cathryn and Anne hold hands. The rest of us walk behind them. We talk about the dodo. Mike had never seen one. "I'm going to paint it," he says.

Wendi huffs. "I was gonna paint it."

"In my painting, he'll be wearing a tie and drinking a martini." Mike laughs, and Cathryn turns around and gives him an eye. She knows that laugh. Since high school she's known it.

"How much have you had?" she says. "I swear to god, Mike, if that handle is gone."

"Excuse me," he says. "Excuse me if I like to have a little fun."

Once Cathryn turns back around, Wendi reaches into the pocket of her swimming trunks and pulls out her flask. She and Mike take turns.

"In my painting, he'll be flying," I say.

"You don't paint," everyone says at once, except Anne, of course, who doesn't know the first thing about me. Anne's ass hangs out of her suit, and her walk is too sure, like she thinks she has this down, this Cathryn thing, like she's permanent here, the most recent fixture. Wendi and Mike and I gulp and giggle.

"Two more weeks, tops," Mike whispers. His guesses are usually the most accurate. He's known her the longest. My skin tingles all of a sudden, part rum, part the image that flashes in my memory; her clothes a pile on the floor, the scratch of Ronald's frail paws on the glass, the stale smoke smell, and the feel of that skin, soft in my palm. Two weeks.

At the swimming hole, we rush the water. It laps our thighs as we sink our way in, getting used to the shock of cool. Submerging my whole body, I forget to hold my breath and rise up coughing. Mike grabs my legs, and I go down again. I open my eyes under the water. Bones litter the lake floor under our feet, many of them ground to form a second layer of sand. We walk all along them without noticing. I let the water carry my legs instead. I swim. When I come up for breath, I'm at the far bank, where Wendi sits atop a rock with her feet skimming the water surface. Her face is red and wet, though her hair is dry.

"You okay?" I ask. A brittle fishbone snaps under my weight.

"I'm okay," she says, shaking her head. "I think I'm in love with her."

Yeah, well, I want to say but don't. I feign surprise. "You're straight, though, right?"

Wendi shrugs. "Does it matter? I hate seeing her like this."

"Happy?" Me too. "Well, if you really loved her, you'd want her happy."

I remember the first time I knew Cathryn wanted it. Wendi, Mike, and me in the car, driving down streets with no names for no reason. Cigarette ash blowing back in through the windows and staining our clothes with the stench. "You're on her list." Mike grinned. "She told me so." Then it was a party at my place, and we snuck into my bedroom and stuffed a chair under the doorknob. The curtains were attached by flimsy little clips and had fallen down, so we put them back up but you could still see through little holes where the fabric was worn, and we did it, aware and uncaring, while partygoer's faces appeared and disappeared like apparitions at each hole in the window, trying to see in.

"You're right," Wendi says, wetting a toe. "What the fuck is wrong with me?"

A school of skeleton fish passes over my feet. Their bone-hard bodies make my hair stand on end. When I stick my head under the water and my eyes adjust, they are already far away, but bringing up their rear is a phantom shiner with the last vestige of its transparent orange scales intact.

"Huh," I say when I bring my head again above water. "I thought those had fully skeletoned a while ago."

"This water freaks me out." Wendi stands and turns, and we both see the leopard this time, its body stretched across a rock in the sun, its rib bones now visible. Wendi's closer to it than me, and I wish we could trade places as she steps toward it until she is so close, she can touch it if she wants. She reaches her hand out. She pulls it back. She helps me out of the water. Together we run back to camp.

WHEN THE GANG RETURNS FROM the swimming hole, Mike has a saber-tooth skeleton at his side, around its neck a collar he has made from the drawstring of his swimming trunks, which now hang below his navel. To keep them on he walks bow-legged, and once he arrives at the fire, he hands Wendi the end of the string and disappears into the tent to change.

Wendi and I have been silent, passing a notebook of portable haikus back and forth, each of us writing one page. It's a game we all used to play. The haikus are nonsensical, the language of ridiculousness. When Mike comes back out, we put the notebook away.

"This is Tegan," he says. "I'm gonna take her home with me."

"Another pet?" Wendi asks. A whole wall of Mike's room is covered in aquariums already. "Dude, you can't breathe in your room as is."

"I hate that name," the saber says. "Give me another one."

"Okay, your name is Nimrod."

"Another one."

"Tilly?" Mike says.

The saber shrugs.

"Tigger?"

The saber snaps Mike's hand. Its teeth draw blood. He slaps its head. The bones rattle. He marches to a tree and ties the saber up, then wraps a dishcloth around his hand. As we eat peanut butter sandwiches and take shots of wine, the saber shouts insults. "Morons," it says, "you don't know shit about life. You think you know everything, but you're fucking clueless."

Mike hits it over the head with an unburnt log. No one screams; it happens too fast. The saber's body falls. Mike unties it and carries it to the river. I follow him, try to tell him to stop, but my voice catches. He tosses the bones in the river and wipes the dirt from his jeans; on top of the dried paint, the stain looks like a skewed portrait, blue eyes and lips and all the rest dirt.

After walking back in silence, we find Cathryn holding the lucky girl, visibly shaken.

"Fucking thing was reminding me of my parents," Mike says.

Cathryn doesn't even bother to shoot Mike the eye. She takes Anne by the hand and leads her to the tent, and when we hear the click of the lock on the tent doors, Mike grabs hold of the wine, opens his throat, and guzzles. I sit beside Wendi and the fire and we don't say a word. The bottle empty, Mike drops into the dirt and rolls back and forth, moving his arms in angel shapes. "I'm sorry," he says again and again. Wendi and I don't comfort him. The firewood crumbles like the bones and we just look on. I'm used to looking and not touching, staying out of the way until it's my turn. I know that Anne won't want us after this, won't want to be a part of this, and somehow it doesn't seem to matter. Two weeks tops, Mike said. He was wrong. It'll go back to normal before that. We'll forget it ever happened, starting tomorrow when we're back in the concrete world.

We sleep the way we are.

ON THE WAY OUT THE next morning we drive across the bridge over the river. In the backseat I stare out the window, and from the water's edge the leopard stares at me. As it pads to shore I notice its legs, all skeleton now. I imagine its claws, invisible but deadly.

The whole ride no one says a word.

When Cathryn and I get back to her place, the skeletons are still in the tank. The T-Rex claws at the glass. His bones creak. "Let me free," he says. I knock on the glass, and Thelma and Louise scurry to the back. Ronald doesn't move, static in his pleading.

Cathryn disappears into the bathroom. I look around her room, at the mess she's left of clothes scattered over the ground. It's hard to see the floor. I groan as I tiptoe over the piles. I reach my hand into the tank and pick the skeleton up by his shoulders. He falls apart in my hands. I carry his bones outside and look across her big backyard, which we only enter to smoke brief cigarettes at night when we need the air. In the back of the yard is an abandoned raised bed, one we all built together when we had nothing but time on our hands, then forgot about it, and I lay Ronald down amongst the dead tomato plants, their thin spines snapped so that they seem to bow as we approach. His bones scatter in the dirt. I shake a plant. Its brittle leaves fall from the branches and bury him.

My profound (working) theory is that the skeletons are a metaphor for SECRETS.

CLAIRE'S PAPA DOESN'T KNOW HER anymore. When they sit for dinner, he pushes his bowl of chili onto the floor. The bowl is plastic; after the first four times, she learned her lesson, but still, it cracks as it hits the tile. The beans spread in a puddle beneath his feet.

"I won't eat your poison," he says.

"It's not poison, Papa. See." She eats a spoonful from her own bowl. "Aren't you hungry?"

"Not hungry enough."

Papa crosses his arms, surveys the rest of the table. It's a long table with twelve chairs, and before each chair a place is set. The phantoms will arrive soon, and when they do—Claire hopes—her father will eat. He always eats with the phantoms around.

In the kitchen, the fluorescent light flickers. The flicker registers as a flash in the corner of Claire's eye in the dining room, a minor annoyance but enough to drive her mad night after night. She needs to fix the light but has little time for household chores. Too much else to do. Clean and cook and try to convince Papa to take his pills.

Claire goes into the kitchen to fill bowls for the phantoms. With the chessboard floor tiles below and the flashing light above, she feels like she's in a game, one of those video games maybe, the kind that comes with a warning: may cause seizures. She hurries, takes a bowl out for each place at the table and sets it atop the placemat. She fills the water glasses with wine and the wine glasses with water. She pulls the bread from the oven and covers the basket with a cloth, places it in the middle of the table. The phantoms won't eat the bread, but they'll devour the butter, leaving greasy stains all over her mother's white tablecloth. Claire places another bowl of chili before Papa. He doesn't touch it.

The phantoms come in through the walls, passing through the plaster and pink puffs of insulation as Claire imagines ghosts would. They look like silhouettes of people Claire may have met before, vaguely familiar in the outlines of their bodies. They take their places at the table. As they pull the chairs out, wood scrapes wood. Already, rivulets dig in the floor. Claire will have to replace the floor if she ever wants to sell the house, after Papa goes. And the lights. Of course, she'll have to fix those lights.

The phantoms eat with their mouths open, grey light pouring from behind their teeth, surprisingly white in their shadow faces. If Claire ever touches the light, she imagines it would burn skin. She never touches the phantoms.

They speak in deep voices, shaky as old men, and they speak often. Every night the same conversations.

"I was only twelve, and the man came to bring us our milk. He had a streak of black in his blonde hair, and I asked him what was the matter with his hair. He leered at me, always leering at me. I thought he was the devil," says one.

"Was he the devil?" asks another.

"Of course he wasn't. What are you, crazy?"

It's hard for Claire to place the voices to the mouths, for they talk even when their mouths are full of food. Chili drips down their chins. Outside the dogs bark at the door. The phantoms don't like dogs. They made that clear.

"What are those blasted noises?" Papa asks. "Can't a man eat his dinner in peace?"

Claire fixes another bowl and places it outside for them. They're Claire's dogs. They were her girlfriend's, before she left them and everything but her books and a brief note, another relic. Papa liked Claire's girlfriend more than he liked Claire. He used to call her Madeline, though her name was Anne. He liked her, he said, because she was funny. Claire has never been funny, and she suspects her father sees too much of him in her, that it confuses him. Anne was a blank slate, but too blank, it turned out; she absorbed too much. She couldn't take it, watching someone go like Papa. Claire never thought she should have to.

Now Claire lives alone with her father, and each night they dine with phantoms. Claire never asked them to be her guests. She isn't quite sure why they're there, in fact. She wants them to leave. Cooking for so many is expensive; it's hard enough when half of what her father eats ends up on the floor.

The truth is that the phantoms comfort him. When they're there, he seems less confused, less angry. He eats his dinner to the last bite. He laughs and tells stories. Makes it seem like the rest of the day was just a nightmare. Claire wants them to leave. She wants them to take her father with them.

It's a horrible thought she has more and more these days.

THE FIRST TIME THE PHANTOMS came for dinner, there were fewer. Four months ago, right before Anne left. That night the fridge had nearly been empty, and Claire too tired after working her shift at the cemetery—she did ground maintenance there, in that silent paradise—to go to the store. She cooked what she could. Vermicelli spring rolls with peanut sauce, spaghetti with canned Alfredo, onion rolls two days past the expiration date. She cooked a lot of food without thinking; once she was in the hang of it, she didn't want to stop cooking. When she stopped, she would have to serve it. She would have to explain again to Papa that this was his home now, and this was dinner. She cooked so much.

Then, the phantoms came to eat it.

Walking into the dining room with Papa's plate in her hand, she saw the first one. It was only a shapeless body and a head made of black mist like car exhaust. The elbows that seemed to rest on the tabletop were of a thicker consistency, nearly solid. Claire made out an indistinct hum, like the low static of a television left on. Then, she noticed there were more of them, three seats full, and her father seemed to be listening to something they were saying that only he could hear. She did what she could; she brought them plates.

After a couple of nights, their bodies began to turn as solid as their elbows, and Claire could hear their words like whispers. Unintelligible but full of inflection, hidden meanings she was sure. She tried harder. Every now and again she picked out a word: house, third, remember. Papa, it seemed, heard them as if they were part of him. Even when Claire heard nothing, he responded, and the phantoms bowed their heads and moved the holes that Claire came to call their mouths.

They were rude guests. They slurped their soup. Bits of food flew from their forks across the table. Claire cleaned up when they left. The phantoms always left through the walls as well, but they never went through the kitchen.

"It's the lights," Papa said. "You got to fix those damn lights."

ANNE HAD ALWAYS FIXED THE broken things. When the florescent lights in Papa's room went out, Anne carried in the ladder from the garage and changed them. She changed the oil in Claire's car, bought a new hose for the washer. She knew how to do things like that. Claire had never been taught. She'd never been motivated to teach herself.

"I can't," Anne said the night before she left. "If we can't fix us, who will?"

They were in bed together, their clothes bunched at their feet, the blankets fallen to the floor. Their breath had steadied. The air in the room was stale in the absence of their sweat. That staleness had hung there, nameless, for weeks. It was overdue that Anne should mention it.

"I know what you'll say when I go. That I couldn't handle this whole situation, with your dad and all. But that's not it, Claire, and I think you know that."

"Right," Claire said, turning away. "Sure I do."

"If you won't talk to me, if you won't try. How can I help you if you won't talk to me about it?"

Anne tried to touch her, but she shrugged Anne off. It was this way no matter what. Claire wanted so badly to talk, but she swallowed it. It had to wait, until later, until later again, until later became months and the words she'd swallowed hardened like lead in her belly. There was no bringing them up again.

In the morning Anne packed the few things she kept there and left while Claire pretended to sleep. Once Claire heard the click of the front door, she wrapped her arms around her knees and rocked in bed.

The anger came later, though it was brief and soon replaced by the acquiescence of a caregiver, taking in events as they rushed forward to meet her. Swallowing them. Keeping them down with soda water and starch crackers, like the sick do.

"WHO IN THE HELL IS this?" Papa asked when he first met Anne. "What in the hell does she want?"

"This is Anne, Papa. She's my girlfriend," Claire said.

Anne shook his limp hand. He had always said that women should not shake hands.

"She looks like a man," Papa said.

Anne didn't look like a man. She had short hair, that was all, cut to her ears, black. Her skin was dark, her eyes brown. She wore black pants and a button-up purple blouse with a collar, a grey pea coat. Claire always thought she looked like she stepped out from a painting faded with age. It fit, because Anne was an artist of the digital era. She designed websites.

"It's nice to meet you, Mr. Pierce." Anne took her hand back but didn't look away from Papa. He was forced to smile.

"Are you here to bring me my lunch, Ms. Madeline?" he asked. "I'll take a tuna sandwich on rye."

In the kitchen, Claire apologized. Her father wasn't always mean, she said, it was the disease. It brought something out that Claire had never seen before, only heard in a rumor from her mother, of her papa's temperament before she was born. A temperament that supposedly evaporated when he became a father. Claire's mother, before her death, always spoke of his transformation like it came from God. Claire didn't believe in God. Anne did. That was another reason Papa came to love her.

What he didn't tell Claire about Anne was that she reminded him of his own wife, three years deceased. She had the same laugh, the same way of moving through the room as if she'd been there all along. He knew this about her when they first met, but as time dragged on, he lost the chance to say it. He lost the memory as he'd lost his wife.

When she'd first gone, his wife, Claire's mother, Papa had not cried. Rather, he felt a strange constriction in his chest that kept him from holding Claire close. He stayed in his chair, looking out the window, a book in his hand so he could claim he was busy if anyone tried to talk. Visitors. They came in droves, left casseroles on the kitchen counter, if Claire was there to let them in. If not, they left the steaming dishes on the front steps for Claire to bring in the next time she came to visit.

That was when the house had been his. It was not his any longer. He didn't know the pictures hung on the wall; he couldn't place the little striped bag in the bathroom or the light blue towel on the rack. The food in the fridge was foreign, exotic. All he wanted was a basket of fried pickles, but the woman in his house— she seemed so familiar—refused.

"Bad for your health," she said. "Here, Papa, eat this."

She called him that, and perhaps he was that to her, but she was not his daughter. He couldn't place her, but he knew this woman, so much older than the bits of Claire he could recall, did not belong to him.

It came and went. Then it went and never came back.

One night a phantom apologizes.

"I'm sorry. I should have been there better for you. I did wrong by you."

Claire has served a new kind of soup, French Onion, which she hopes Papa will appreciate more than chili. She doesn't look up at the phantom; he's sitting at the far end of the table and is easy to ignore. But his words confuse her. Sometimes they do that. They speak like her papa. They relay pieces of him he seems to have lost.

When she first noticed that they knew so much of the inside of his mind, she wished that they would give it all back. She's given up on hopes like that. Now the only wish is the one she's afraid and ashamed to admit. *Take him. Take him, please. Take him with you.*

"I should have told you it was going to be okay. All those words you probably needed to hear, I didn't give them to you," the phantom says.

Claire looks up at Papa. His expression is blank as he spoons French Onion soup into his mouth. He doesn't look at her, though she sees him see her from the corner of his eye.

"Should've let you know I still loved you, even though you looked so much like her. Reminded me of her."

Finally, Claire stands from the table. Without a word, she walks to her bedroom. She needs a moment to breathe. It would have been a welcome apology from her father's throat. From a ghost of a memory, she never wanted to hear anything so personal. The words creep through her skin. She shivers. On the edge of her bed, she tries not to start shaking, but she has to grab hold of the nightstand to steady her hands.

There, on the stand, is one of the books Claire can never read again. Anne used to read it to her before bed. It's a book about the history of the movies, but it may as well have been a book of lullabies for how Anne's voice smoothed the words. Claire can't look at it. She ought to get rid of it, but she can't bear to touch it. In the DVD player, there's a movie Claire can't make herself remove.

Alone in the bedroom, Claire hears voices from the dining room as clear as if they were there with her. They could be coming through the vents, but she doubts that's the case. She lies across the bed and unbuttons her shirt, wriggles out of her jeans. The cotton sheets against her skin is soothing. The air from the fan blows down on her, though never will either feel as soothing as Anne's hands, or her mother's.

Eventually, Claire will have to get up from the bed. She will have to go back into the dining room and clean up the mess. For now, she will let the room take care of him. She will let the phantoms comfort him. She closes her eyes and thinks about her mother, the way she flipped her hair back to clear it from her face. Her white white teeth, the rare smile, less rare when she and Claire were alone.

Anne was something like her mother, but her smile was for everybody. It was what Claire liked most.

Claire rolls over face down on the pillows. They smell like fresh laundry. Claire's breath catches. They will never smell like Anne again. She's washed it away. It's a step she hadn't thought she'd taken, and the pressure building in her chest tells her it's a step she wasn't ready for. How could she have done that without noticing? She curls against the pillows and makes herself cry, for Anne, for her mother, her papa, her everyone.

THINGS CLAIRE CANNOT TOUCH FOR fear of losing them:

1. The CD she made for Anne but never gave her.
2. The books, mostly on the bottom shelf, all gifts.
3. Her mother's old silver-plated mirror and comb.
4. The pillowcases she won't wash again.

5. The recipes in the recipe box, written in her mother's hand, one in Anne's. Her father's scratchy instructions for a "secret tortilla soup." Food she can no longer eat.

6. The dirty pair of underwear Anne forgot beneath the bed.

7. The bandages Anne bought to bind the burn on Claire's hand from cooking.

8. Her father's Christmas trinkets, still up from December.

9. Her father's photo album, full of blank spaces.

10. Her father's hand.

PAPA NEVER WAS ONE FOR apologies, for feelings. None of them were.

Here was Claire, the past: an open letter in her hand. She bounded into the kitchen, where her mother stood at the stove. The smell of fish frying, the greasy scent of hot oil, caught Claire at the threshold. She paused only a moment before she waved the letter through the air.

"I got in!" she yelled.

Her mother turned, smiled, turned back to the stove. "That's great, dear."

As if her excitement were a balloon suddenly popped, the air wheezed away. Claire stood with a letter in her hand, unsure. Tossed the letter on the table.

Despite her initial excitement, after a semester Claire dropped out.

Instead, she held as many odd jobs as she could until she happened on the cemetery position. Claire's been there now for fifteen years. Without a home to call her own, the cemetery grounds become the place she most likes to be. There, she can fix things. When the grass gets too long, she cuts it. When the flowers die, she replaces them. When she happens upon someone crying, she in no way feels obligated to comfort them. Her place is in the background of their lives, safe.

Being the center of Anne's life made her uncomfortable. Always, she felt on edge, her limbs rigid, her back tight. Anne tried to massage the knots away, but it didn't work, because when Anne's hands left her skin, the knots returned. She didn't know how to explain this, to tell Anne it wasn't her fault.

Claire can't remember ever seeing her parents kiss. She can't remember them kissing her. Now, in her bedroom, she does not remember Anne's lips.

IT WASN'T A SURPRISE WHEN the doctor called Claire and told her she would have to find care for her father. Her father had been forgetting; it started when her mother was sick and worsened after the funeral. Little things. When Claire called, he told her the same story in the course of thirty minutes. He forgot where he put his wallet. Claire became the caretaker of his credit cards, as he could no longer keep track of the payments. He wrote bad checks.

Then, he forgot where he was. He asked for his mother, long passed. The first people he forgot were insignificant: actors, politicians, cousins who never visited. Then it was the postman, and his nephew who visited. Finally, it was Claire, as the doctors had warned.

"Where's my little girl?" he asked, and she would explain. She explained again. At first it was temporary; it did, eventually, come back to him. "Claire," he said, squeezing her hand. "You're back. I sure do like it when you visit."

"Of course, Papa," Claire said. "Don't worry, I won't stop visiting you."

The memory of her mother, on the other hand, was harder for him to lose. It seemed as if, though it too came and went, it was more often present. He remembered her, but her absence was something he couldn't explain to himself. He asked about her all the time back then.

These days, he doesn't ask about her at all. Claire envies him his ignorance.

Claire didn't move in right away. At first, she hired caregivers to stay with him 24/7. Then the money ran out, the savings dried up, the cards maxed out. Social security and Medicaid paid for only half the care, and Claire didn't make enough to pay the rest. She broke the lease on her apartment and moved back in.

Anne came along later, at Claire's yard sale. She'd cleaned out Papa's old things, antiques he let rot in the garage, a bicycle missing its tire, the clothes he no longer wore—these days he mostly donned his favorite blue robe and plaid pajamas. Anne wasn't really interested in the merchandise, but she bought the bike so she could talk to Claire. She arranged to pick it up later when she wasn't on her way to the store. She lived in the neighborhood, she explained. Claire thought she talked too much, a trait she would learn to love.

Now she misses the voice. Silence fills the empty air. Except when the phantoms come and take it, and there is no comfort in their stolen words.

●●

THE STORIES THE PHANTOMS TELL are familiar to Claire. Every night at dinner she feels nostalgic with each mouthful of chili, and it isn't the food, though that too comes from a memory of limbo years with a crockpot and three cans of beans. She likes the nostalgia of taste buds. What falls from the phantoms' mouths, she likes much less.

Papa told her some of the stories the phantoms have adopted, and her mother told her others. The rest are new to her, but they ring with her father's voice. She hates hearing her father's words from so many grey mouths. She hates not being able to look at him when she responds. He finds the phantoms entertaining; the stories are new to him.

The evening of the apology, once Claire returns to the dining room, she finds her father still there, his guests gone.

"It's time to go," he says.

"Okay," says Claire. She moves to help him, wraps her arm around his arm. "Let's go to bed now, Papa."

"No." He jerks his arm away. She thinks she knows what's coming next; he will throw a fit, tell her to leave him alone, tell her to take him where he belongs.

But he doesn't. Instead he looks at the wall, the spot from which the phantoms leave. Claire looks there as well. One of the phantoms is still on this side of the wall. It extends a grey arm. "Time to go."

Her papa pats the table. "Be right back," he says. Suddenly Claire knows it's a lie. She can't explain how she knows it. Her father will go, and he won't come back.

She leads her father by the hand. The shadow consumes him, his arm, his shoulder. It pulls his body forward, and together he and the phantom walk through the wall. Through the plaster Claire hears her father's voice. "Those damn lights. Hope she remembers."

Once he's gone, Claire can't quite move. She stares at the spot where he stood. It was sudden, she thinks, more so than she thought it would be. She's not quite sure—she has to consider what has happened—if she's had time to build herself up to this. If she'll be able to get through this without anyone anymore to call hers. She wraps her arms around her chest. The room is cold. The dogs outside howl. She lets them in. There is some vague kind of comfort in their fur. They lick the smell of chili from her hand.

Once they've settled down, she goes into the kitchen, pours the soup into a plastic container, slides the container into the fridge. She rinses the dishes and loads the washer. Stands on the cabinet and tries to pull down the light cover. The side cracks in her hands, and a shard of glass crashes to the chessboard floor. Like a pawn, she thinks, too small to be significant. Back on the floor, she moves the glass from square to square. Crumbs dig into the palms of her hands. One square at a time, she slides the glass to the edge of the kitchen, then over, into the dining room. She considers picking it up, throwing it away, but she doesn't. She crosses her legs where she is and waits to see if the light will stop flickering, if her father will after all come back.

As for Anne, there's a phone and a number. Claire still remembers, after all.

"The first order of business," Anne says once Claire lets her in, "is that light."

Claire has already thrown away the glass on the floor. She's already cooked a pan of tomatillo enchiladas for them to eat for dinner. The table she has set for two.

"Okay," Claire says.

It's really all that need be said.

THE WILL STATED THAT THE sisters split the house and its contents 50/50, but it is impossible to cut a house in half. ← *Bill Hunker would beg to differ*

"I grew up in this house," Jackie said, seated across from Beth at the dinner table Jackie had helped their dad build when she was eleven. Beth had long ago gone off to college; that had been the year of Jackie's first kiss, the year of a flooded downstairs bathroom, the year of a police phone call in the night and an impromptu emptying of savings to pay bail for Beth's public intoxication charge. "You weren't raised here. You don't know what this place means to me."

"Sentimentality won't pay bills, Jackie. I know the house means a lot to you, but we're in debt. Things change when you have a family. Your priorities shift." Beth pushed her black hair over her shoulder. It was the same black as Jackie's hair with the same silk shine. Everyone who saw them knew they were sisters right away. "And you're about to start your own life, you know. The money from the house could pay for grad school. It could be a down payment on a house of your own."

"I don't need grad school," Jackie said.

"But if your music doesn't work out."

Jackie stared into the cup of green tea she'd let get cold. If her music didn't work out. It would happen for her; there had never been any other option.

"Maybe, if you could pay me my half, we could work it out," Beth said. "But how would you afford to pay me? The house is worth three hundred grand, at least. Then there's the land ...." Her forehead wrinkled. "I feel bad for you, I do, but what would you do with a house this big?"

Where the sisters sat, ill family dogs had once hid beneath the chair skirts. Boys had come to dinner, then girls, to impress the family, to be impressed. There had been stoned family occasions where Beth or Jackie, never the both of them, had snuck a joint beforehand then tried to pretend as though her eyes weren't struggling to stay open.

The house didn't want to be given away. It had grown accustomed to the family. It was sad to no longer hear the thump of footsteps daily across the wood floors or the laughter of the mother, solid and hearty, or the boisterous snores of the father. Their voices, gone, were now replaced with the familiar bickering of siblings, the girls who, one by one, had abandoned their rooms and gone off on adventures they didn't bother to tell the house about. At least they left slowly, gathering their things bit by bit, the youngest not even fully moved on, several of her belongings still shoved in an upstairs closet. The older ones, the mother and father, their absence was too sudden. One day they were here, the next gone, and no explanation had been given as to why. It was maddening, the not knowing, the being a house. But the house understood one thing, and that was that its days might be numbered. That, without the memory-holders under its roof, the house might lose itself and forget all it ever knew.

"What about the house?" Jackie asked. "Could you bear to have some strangers scraping up the floors, painting the walls, cutting down the trees?"

Beth looked around the dining room. "The walls need painting. This brown is god-awful."

The house wished it could do that wailing thing the people did sometimes. It wished it could leak through the walls like it had sometimes when the older ones still lived there, but neither sister had turned a single of its faucets on for weeks, and to break the pipes without the pressure of running water was difficult for the house.

Jackie's footsteps thumped through the hall and down the stairs. Her bedroom door slammed.

At the kitchen table, Beth buried her face in her cupped palms and cried quiet as foundation shifting.

ONCE THE HOUSE WAS ABLE to calm itself, to eat the energy that seeped from the sisters, one's rigid sorrow, the other's unadulterated grief that flowed from her like banshee screams, it was able to create the apparitions. Every day the sisters arrived at the house to protect their territory, but when they returned each evening to homes that the house envied for their permanent occupancy, the house forced shadows from the walls. At first, they remained the shapes of the objects from which they came: the square of a painting, the tall stick of a coat hanger with a dusty coat hanging from it, a chair with three legs. With practice, the house found that it was able to contort the shadows into shapes more to its liking.

A man. A woman. Hands intertwined as they walked through the halls. Merging into a kiss before the stovetop where the man stood for half an hour before traveling into the dining room, before taking his seat at the dining room table, before the woman joined him there. The house could not imitate the screech of chairs moving against its skin, and it could not recreate the thumps of feet against its floors, but it could keep the company of shadows.

BECAUSE SHE COULD NOT STAND the smell of an unoccupied house, upon her next visit, Jackie gathered the ingredients for bread from the cabinets, where they had sat since her parents' accident. She measured the flour, letting the excess fall onto the pristine countertops. The house deserved to look lived in. It needed to look lived in. Maybe then Beth would feel more at home here, would not be so keen on throwing away all that was left of their parents. When the dough was mixed, she rolled it into a ball and kneaded it into the granite countertop. Her knuckles sank down into the dough. The warm pressure of Jackie's fist made the house shiver and creak. When Jackie was finished, her hands covered in dough, she placed the dough in a bowl to rise and washed up. The sticky residue swirled down the drain and caught in the house's pipes.

When the bread was done baking, she removed it from the oven and pressed her hands across the smooth, warm top of the loaf. The top felt like soft granite, as smooth and as perfect, as absent of mistakes. She pressed her cheek against it. When it was no longer warm on her skin, she pulled herself up and looked down into the mild imprint of her face. Her sister's face. Her mother's face. The dough indistinct enough to be mistaken for any for them.

BETH AVOIDED THE KITCHEN. IT was the one place she had never liked to go, as any time she ventured there as a child she was asked to help with dishes, with cooking, with wiping down the countertops. The kitchen was where her father would go again and again to the liquor cabinet, where she heard the clink of ice in a glass. Her sister was never asked to do a chore. By the time Jackie was born, the family had changed. There was no alcohol. There were no screaming matches between mother and father. There were no fist-sized holes in the walls. No belts on skin. And Jackie never knew what she had been lucky enough to miss.

The old bedroom where Beth used to find solace was the only place for which Beth thought she would pine. The house had never liked Beth as much; always, she had been like a ghost within its walls, a living version of the shadow people who now hid when the sisters arrived. As a teenager, she lit candles on its floor close to the hanging fabric of her bed sheet. She never cared enough to vacuum the carpet in her bedroom, and the house felt its grunge for years, until she moved away and the mother called in the cleaning company.

Beth stood now in the doorway, her arms crossed, looking at her old bed, and she felt nostalgic for the ugly off-white walls, for the chipped light switch and the lopsided fan that whomped as it rotated. She had fallen into the bed after nights of high school parties, with her friends up all night giggling into the dark, with the first woman she made love to, with the first man.

But then, the bed had also been soaked with the sweat of fever, with the salt of tears that fell in her sleep, with the shrill of night terror screams upon waking.

The house did not know the difference. The house wanted to be loved. For a moment, it thought Beth would give it that without asking for something in return. But she would not. As for Jackie, her love for the house wouldn't be enough to save it. That much the house knew like it knew it was made from pier-and-beam, from concrete and fluffy pink insulation, from wood and granite and carpet fibers. A terrible truth; it would never be skin. But it could witness skin. The house wanted Beth and Jackie to stay. Beth and Jackie would stay, if it was the last thing the house did.

THE FIRST TIME BETH AND Jackie saw the shadows, the sisters were fighting. Another conversation about the house had led to sour words that they spit at one another like sunflower seed husks. It was maddening to them both that the other could not see that they were losing themselves to a house.

The sisters stood in the living room with the lights off. Beth had arrived to find Jackie cross-legged on the floor, studying the ceiling, her violin at her side.

"What are you up to?" Beth asked.

"You don't even care that our parents are dead, do you?" Jackie said.

Beth's stomach flipped. "That is ridiculous. You're being ridiculous."

"This house is all we have left of them, and you want to sell it, all so you can keep living in an expensive house you can't even afford. A house that you constantly complain about. Every other week you say you want to move somewhere new. You've never wanted to stay in one place for any length of time, and all of a sudden you just have to sell this house so you can pay off the one you supposedly love living in." Jackie stomped her foot. She knew it was childish, but she feared if she didn't release the energy somehow, she would lose her mind.

"What the fuck is wrong with you? You're just a child. When you're older—"

"I'm me! I'm going to stay me even when I'm your age. I'm not just going to suddenly turn into you. I'm different, Beth. I won't ever understand this, and I won't ever forgive you. You're the meanest sister anyone could ever have." Jackie collapsed onto the couch, cradling her body in her arms. Beth stood, arms crossed, and stared at her younger sister, always prone to emotional outbursts, defensive and sensitive. Beth didn't want to argue anymore. She wanted it to be over so they could live without their parents' deaths looming over their head, so they could move on, the way adults were supposed to do.

The shadows glided through the room with hands clasped between them. The windows rattled. The wood floor went cold.

Beth and Jackie watched as their parents' shadows passed them by. Once the shadows had traveled through the kitchen and into the dark of a hallway that Beth and Jackie couldn't see, Jackie unfolded herself and called out.

"Mom, Dad, where you are going?"

Jackie rose and took one step. Beth held her hand across Jackie's chest.

"Stay here," Beth said. "I'll go."

Beth walked down the hall but didn't dare to flip on the lights. Shadows changed in the light. She looked into the bathroom, but it was empty. She peered into the guest room, but it too was clear of all shadows but the one from a tree outside the window that moved on the other side of the glass. She went down the stairs, and in the room to the right, her parents' old bedroom, she found the shadows asleep beneath the blankets, their translucent black heads upon the white of the pillows.

"Are you awake?" she whispered, as she had as a child, in another house, before she'd known better.

The shadows stirred. One beckoned her forward. She walked to the end of the bed, crawled atop the blankets, and lay between them, though she didn't dare pull the covers over her body. When Jackie finally worked up the nerve to check on her sister, she found her asleep in an empty bed.

"Maybe we should sell it," Jackie said during their next discussion. She sat on the porch outside. Since she'd seen the shadows, she'd found it difficult to be inside. The house creaked and moaned, and the shadows moved but never seemed to pay her any notice. It was Beth they clung to, Beth they invited into their bed each night. Beth's husband was beginning to worry; she hadn't been home in three days. Arthur had asked to come with Beth, to help with the cleaning out of the house, but Beth told him he'd better not. Better for their son that he stay.

The house wanted a child. It remembered the word, remembered the joy that children brought. Remembered how they became adults who returned again and again. It remembered how persuasive they could be, how they could convince people to stay and love them. It could learn from a child.

"We can't sell it now. They want something. They need something. We have to work at getting them to tell us what that is." Beth chewed her fingernail. "What if they want to apologize to me? What if they need closure?"

"Beth, I don't think that's Mom and Dad." Jackie looked out at the winter trees, their skeleton branches like fingers stretching to the sky. "I don't know what it is, but it isn't our parents."

"You don't know that for sure."

"You're right. I don't. But it doesn't feel right. Why wouldn't they acknowledge me, too?"

How, the house wondered, could it make the child come?

AFTER THE SHADOWS, JACKIE FELT free to leave the house, to leave Beth to do whatever she might do in Jackie's absence. Within the walls of Jackie's own apartment, the walls that once paled in familiarity to the house's warmth, she felt at home, as if she were wrapped, even when she was not, in the comfort of her weighted blanket. The blank walls became more soothing to her than the colored walls decorated with squares of art at her parents' house, the house that now sent a shiver down her spine when she thought of it.

Beth felt, when she was not inside the house, as though her skin were coming apart, as if she were disintegrating from the inside out. At her home, she shook in bed as she dreamt of shadows cradling her adult body in their arms, hoisting her over their heads as she had once done for her four-year-old son, Logan, the same son who now asked her, again and again, *What's wrong?*

She had no answer for him. She diverted his attention with his favorite action figures. His question haunted her. She stayed in the house at first to find the answer, then to avoid the question, then because she forgot altogether that she had any other place to be.

In her old room, Beth felt a strange urge to pull the toys her parents had stowed for Logan out onto the floor and rummage through them as though she had once played as a child in the house, but she had never been a child in that house at all. She was ten when her parents had moved her there, too old for the dolls that she packed nonetheless then left in their boxes in her closet. Now she ripped open the boxes and dumped dolls across the carpet, dressed and undressed them, moved their bodies across the walls. The shadows stood in the doorway and watched.

Finally, Beth's husband declared it necessary to go out there himself, to bring the boy along. Jackie begged him not to go; Jackie could not bear to watch her nephew's face when Logan saw what had become of his mother. Arthur listened at first, but their house needed its own mother, its own wife, its own Beth.

When he arrived, Jackie sat on the top step of the stairwell leading into the house.

"I don't feel safe anywhere else here," she said. "If I were you, I would stay on the porch with me."

"You come inside, Aunt Jackie," said Logan, pulling at her arm. "I want to tell Mom about my new Lego set."

"Later," Jackie said. "I'll come in later."

Inside the house, Arthur smelled vegetables rotting in an abandoned compost and air stale from not opening a single window since the accident. Logan tiptoed into the hall, pulled to his mother through the dark. When he found her in her old room, playing with dolls, he ran to her and threw his arms around her neck.

"Can I play with you?" he asked as he pulled back. The dolls looked like mirror images of her, each of them with the same black hair. He wanted no more than to play with her replicas, to play with her. With all the dolls surrounding them, there was so much of her here when there had been so little of her lately. He wanted to be with her for as long as she would let him, for he knew, or thought he knew, that she was not the mother he had last seen. That she would not want him at her side like she used to.

But the house. Logan could feel that the house wanted him.

Arthur, too, felt welcomed by the house as his bare feet padded across the carpet. A surge of warmth like a tongue rippled inside him. It had been three months since Beth's hands trailed the hairs of his body.

Arthur and Logan did not see the shadows until the shadows were sure that these new people would not run from them. Then they emerged from the walls, peeling themselves from the dusty space beneath picture frames. They wrapped themselves around Logan's little body and covered him in shadow. They wanted to spread, wanted to consume this family that oozed grief like an infection.

The house watched the shadows and knew that it had lost its hold on them. The house had been distracted by the presence of two more bodies beneath its roof. The shadows had wants of their own. The house had not considered that.

It tried to suck the shadows back into its floor as it did with spilled water, but they had made the little boy one of them.

The house would not sacrifice the little boy. Perhaps there was a way to bring him back from shadow. The house creaked its floorboards and watched as Beth looked up from her dolls, as she reached toward her shadow son. So, the living could be shadow, too. If Beth were shadow, she could speak to her mother, her father; the boundary between shadow and skin was what separated them, what made it impossible for them to tell her what they wanted.

Beneath the shadow, Logan still loved her. It was as though he were sleeping, dreaming one of his scary dreams. He moved only if the shadow let him move. He fell toward his mother. She took him in her arms. The shadows shivered at the warmth. Yes, they thought, yes. So hungry, so empty. They filled themselves with Beth.

Beth opened her mouth. The shadows flowed in over her tongue like winter air. A great dizziness slowed her heartbeat. Arthur, she remembered, her thoughts hazy, as though she were high, like she used to get. Hands, the shadows thought. Touch.

Outside, on the porch, Jackie heard nothing but shrieking cicadas shedding their exoskeletons in the trees. She played their shedding songs back to them.

Once Jackie's song had ended and she once more dared to enter the house, she found a scene of shadows.

She walked the rooms as calm and collected as a coroner, but inside she felt a quiet shock. She wanted to throw up, to run, but it was up to her now to get her sister out of there. In Beth's old bedroom, two shadows played with dolls on the floor. In her parents' old bedroom, a shadow writhed atop her parents' quilts. In the living room, two familiar shadows, the ones she had seen pass through this room before, held hands on the couch.

The house warmed its floor as she walked. Please, the house tried to say, help me. The shadows did not comfort the house; they were not what it wanted after all. It wanted skin, blood. It wanted the child back. It wanted the father. It wanted back the parents and the sisters whose bickering filled it with a cacophony more soothing than this silence. The shadows could not last independent of the house; it had to drive them outside, into the light.

The house warmed a path into the kitchen, to the sink. But once Jackie found her way to the kitchen, she went instead to the cabinet above the microwave. She opened the cabinet and saw inside the red shock of a lighter. She pulled it down and ran her fingers over the catch. The flame was warm in her hand. She rubbed her other hand over her bare arms and realized just how cold she had become, gooseflesh prickling, hairs on end, nipples hard as glass.

In her sister's old bedroom, she stepped over shadows and found the candles on the night stand, the very candles her mother used to warn would light the house on fire. She lit them all, set them right beneath the bed, and pulled the blankets down into them.

The bed that Jackie used to sneak into when she was scared and her sister lived at home caught the flame she placed like an offering below it. The armoire Jackie always wanted caught the flame. The books that Jackie used to gaze at, too aware that one day she would die and would never read them all, caught the flame. The fire swept from the bedroom to the living room, catching the wood floor Jackie and Beth used to slide across in their socks. The shadows screeched and flickered their way through the fire. The firelight licked at the walls and altered their shapes. They flickered from flame to flame to the door, where Jackie waited on the other side.

Her nephew bounded first from the door. As the sunlight touched him, he solidified, curdling like spoilt milk, until he was Logan again. Then came her brother-in-law, the transformation from shadow to skin spreading like an infection up his body until his face came into focus.

The house could feel itself crumbling. It felt betrayed by the Jackie sister. It could not believe that she would not try to save it. Its pipes groaned as Jackie stood outside, her fingernail between her teeth, watching the door but not moving to extinguish the flame.

Inside, the sister shadow pulled at two shadows halfway stuck into the wall. They would not budge. They held their open hands over their faces, trying to block out the scene before them, but they could still see flames through the translucence like a mirage in summer heat. The sister pulled and pulled but did not move them.

The house felt like a fool. In the bathroom and the kitchen, it used all its energy to burst its pipes. It wanted to feel the comforting release of its water like the water wailing of its inhabitants. A flood rushed from the cracks and tore through the halls. It soaked the walls. The fire died a noiseless death.

Jackie waited. Then she could wait no longer. The house was no longer aflame; she found her sister flickering from shadow to skin on the living room couch, the house around them broken and wet and singed, smoke hovering across the ceiling.

"Come on," Jackie said. And her sister looked up at her, nodded, rose to her feet, and they walked together, shadow hand in corporal grasp, until they emerged and Beth was herself again, solid and stubborn as ever.

"Mom and Dad," Beth said.

"That wasn't them," Jackie said.

"I know," Beth said. "They're dead."

The house watched through a haze as the sisters wrapped their arms around each other. It knew, without them saying, that it would never see them again. The shadows inside had retreated into ruined walls. The house knew that it would become ash and rubble on the ground, that it would then be built again.

But the house would make sure its people stayed next time. It would not make the same mistake thrice.

something about intergenerational trauma / cycles?

but who is the house?

HUSBAND

Is he addressing a human or an adopted senior dog?

We knew when we met you that we would have to let you go. We wanted you anyway. Even these days, when we come across an item you left behind, your toothbrush buried in the bathroom cabinet, we can't quite figure out what it was about you. Maybe we just wanted someone to hold, new skin. It didn't hurt that you were beautiful. You had a way about you, the most magnetic presence at your cousin's party. All of us trapped inside like that, breathing the same air for so long, no wonder we grew attached. The rain pounded on the roof, you remember this, and all the guests huddled in the living room looking out, wondering when it would stop so we could all go home. The rain ruined everything.

well that answers that

"Damn rain's coming more and more," you said. Your name was Cathryn. We knew that much already. "I would think that means something, 'cept it never really fucking does."

Is there going to be anything redemptive about this because im getting really bad unicorn hunting-esque vibes here

"It means the rain is coming more," I said. "Name's Donovan."

My wife smiled, lowered her eyes. She did this sometimes, when she wanted to play coy. "Heather," she said. "We already know yours. A gorgeous name."

"You're nice," you said. You shook our hands at the same time.

We didn't know what we were getting into. We couldn't have known.

WIFE

What was it like before you came around? I don't remember. It was a while ago. I know what my husband tells me—it was good but unremarkable. I know what the truth is; things were simple back then.

I used to garden. You never knew what that felt like, to touch the soil with your hands. Donovan, he was always a poet. His day job has him working behind a desk in a debtor's office trying to locate relatives to pay the debts of the thousands dead, but I know better. Something about the way he speaks. He never writes a damn word, but once when we were young and drunk, he admitted he composed strings of words in his head. You never knew that about him. We didn't let you know things like that. Was that our mistake? You studied art history at the local college, for fun. That much I won't forget, because you brought me books on Mucha, promised someday to take me to Europe, to pay me back for all I did for you. With so many of our generation gone to rain, you didn't need the degree. You could have done whatever you wanted without one. But you wanted it, and that was enough for you. I should have known better about Europe. You were, after all, just a girl.

My husband was hesitant. That first night at the party, he pulled me into an empty bedroom, shut the door.

"Are you sure about this?" he asked. He had read my eyes. There was a window in the room. The rain banged on the glass. Back then, it scared me. "What if it changes things, for us?"

"That's what I want," I said. "I want to be changed."

He kissed me hard, fast, we couldn't keep you waiting, and we left the room and found you by the buffet. You had a face someone could forget if it was all they saw. You weren't eating. I wondered what you looked like when you ate. I handed you a chocolate éclair. You took it, studied it like I imagine you would one of your paintings. You took a bite. Chocolate lined your lips. You wiped it off with the back of your hand.

"Good," you said. You handed the rest to me. "You finish it."

I had never wanted anything more in my life.

LOVER

I wouldn't have done you like that, either of you, if I didn't think you could handle it. If I wasn't mistaken. About what we wanted from one another. In some ways I wanted you guys as much as you wanted me, and in some ways, I wanted nothing you could give me. Because you gave me a lot, most of it unasked for, and I'll admit I didn't know what to do with it all.

The rain was starting to wig me, and I needed someone to take the rain away. It had been a while since I'd lived with my parents, and I needed someone to hold me and let me know it was all gonna be okay. That the rain was temporary. Neither of you had children. I didn't want to be your children. But I wanted more than lovers.

If you haven't figured it out already, I don't really know what I want.

I'm twenty-two years old. I'm not supposed to live in a world with this kind of rain.

HUSBAND

I think a lot about that night we met. When the rain let up, we slipped our steel boots over our party shoes and left, the three of us, in my wife's old Dodge. She pulled her steel gloves from her dress purse, slipped them on, and opened the doors for us.

"I feel like such a lady," you said.

"Madame Cathryn, your chariot," I said. I was trying to be clever, but I was nervous. You were the sweetest thing I'd seen in a long time. I knew in the back of my mind you never would have come if not for Heather. She had the looks. But you know that already. You know all of this already. I just need to tell it again, to make sure there was nothing I missed. No small detail, no phrase you murmured into our ears as we took that long drive back to our house. The roads were slick, the concrete shiny like a sheet of ice. The trees looming to either side, affected by the rain in only the best of ways, thick and tall as giants. Unlike us, their thick skin could take it. But you know that, too.

Heather drove ten miles per hour with the brights on. The danger wasn't gone. It had rained a lot, and the rain shone bright in our faces in the headlights' glare. You said you felt safe with us. I always hoped that, of all the things you said, that thing was true.

WIFE

Don and I were again able to breathe once we'd got home safe that night. No accidental spray of rain had come in through the car door, the front door. It had been so many years, we were used to the precautions. They felt to us like a habit we could never forget about. I wondered if to you, who had never known anything but, they were as second nature as eating. Removing our shoes, dipping them into the barrel of antidote by the door, for gloves, boots, to soak. Washing our hands with chemical soap, the smell like grape medicine.

Our house was dirty. The floors hadn't been vacuumed that week, and there were smudges of dirt on the tile inside the door from the day before. I apologized. You said the polite thing, that it looked okay to you.

"You're just saying that," I said.

"I'm not, it really does look good." You smiled. It was the smile that always made my stomach jump a little, like the way it used to, bringing home a girl or a boy, before it felt familiar to hold someone's hand. I'll remember that smile even if I've already forgotten your face.

"Really, you don't have to say that." I said.

"I'm serious," you said. "I live in an apartment," you said. "I'm in college," you said.

I remembered what that was like. Dust settled, and you let it settle. You wouldn't even notice, not till you got sick and your mom told you it was dust you must have missed the last time you cleaned. And you laughed, because you wouldn't let your mother come over and she didn't know you hadn't cleaned since you moved in, maybe since that one night when you got too drunk to sleep and couldn't do anything but clean, but that was long ago. I remembered that life, and I was jealous. I wanted to take it from you. I wanted to push you on the bed and suck that life from your bellybutton.

I didn't want to scare you away. But I ached for it. I think you could see it in me. What could I see in you? A curiosity. One I would stroke.

LOVER

When I say that I don't know what I want, I mean the big stuff. I mean life stuff. That first night with you guys, I knew this kind of clarity. It was knowing, right then, what I wanted. I saw myself pressed between two people. Two naked bodies sheltering me from the rain. In my far-reaching fantasy, a place where I was spoken for. I will never work again, I thought, these people will let me live with them and love them. We will love each other so much it will dry us up. I'll admit, I also saw the things you would provide, material stuff my parents refused me: original Kiefer sculptures, instruments to bring out the hidden talent you alone would see in me, booze—I was only twenty then and couldn't buy it myself. It sounds stupid, but it's the truth.

I tell you this so you will know then how naïve I was. And still am, nowhere near the two of you in what I know about the world.

I don't remember a time before the rain. I was too small. You already knew each other when it came. You had friends who were victims of the first wave, before they figured out what was killing them. You probably had close calls yourself, which later you looked back on and cried for. It gave you skin like a shell, so fragile I sometimes feared I might break you.

We never talked about any of this, not in the whole year we were together. Why not? There was a lot in you I never learned from. That was one of my mistakes.

HUSBAND

Once we'd stood around the kitchen and poured our glasses of Malbec, we retired to the living room where we gathered on the couch, you in the middle. It would be that way always. I turned on the stereo, some Pink Floyd, *Wish You Were Here*. You looked surprised.

"What, not what you expected?" I asked.

"No Mozart, or some classy shit?" you asked. "From the size of this house, I expected some classy shit."

When you drank, we came to learn, you spoke like an old-school construction worker. It was one of the things we would learn to call endearing. Until we felt betrayed, and then it turned for us into an unfortunate quality we had been forced to accept.

"This is from the musical golden years, missy."

"It's cool," you said. "I like it."

I can't listen to that song anymore.

It was Heather who kissed you. I've always admired her for that. You were still holding your glass, and you let it rest between your legs so you could press both your hands into her cheeks. I watched, conflicted. I took the glass from between your thighs and put it on the coffee table. I set mine next to it. I unbuttoned your blouse and slipped my hand inside your shirt. My wife gripped your thigh on top of your jeans.

I want to remember this moment, our first. I want to remember how warm you were, how soft the skin, how when you turned and kissed me your mouth was red with wine, and you tasted of alcohol and curses.

"Fuck," my wife said. She was already absorbing you in little ways, like a language. "Fuck, let's go to bed."

Outside the rain began again.

WIFE

I made the first move. Really, you could blame the whole thing on me if you wanted. I took your hand and led you to our bedroom, the bed already unmade, waiting. Where our clothes came off and blended into the pile of laundry on the floor.

It was all the awkwardness of that first time again. I unbuttoned your jeans, and you lifted your torso so I could pull them down over your hips, your legs. They caught at your feet. You laughed, I laughed, and I yanked them off each foot. You lifted your arms, and we slipped the blouse from your body, you didn't wear a bra, and there you were, naked. Your legs pressed together. I stuck my hand between your thighs. Left my clothes on. My husband removed his shirt, his pants, kneeled at your feet.

We kissed you all over.

After, we lay naked and breathless together. I pressed my breasts into your back and felt as though I was pressing our bodies into one. We fell into a sleep so light the rain should've woken us. It didn't. What woke us was the sound of it stopping.

LOVER

Enough. Enough about that night. Never mind that I lay there, in the best sleep of my life, that feeling of safety. Dry warmth. That I knew I would be with the two of you as long as I could stand it. Yeah, I knew it wouldn't be forever. I thought you knew that, too. I never once imagined that you could want it differently. After all, you were married. You had a life together you'd worked out separate from me. There was a picture beside your bed of the two of you at a beach, your hair dark, your skin smooth and firm and red with infatuation, your arms around each other's shoulders like you were competing for control. Heather, you were winning. In the photo you had a power in the way you stood, brute, shoulders squared, and Don's brows were furrowed so slightly that I'm almost sure I'm the only one who ever noticed. It would be impossible for me to tap into that history, to ever catch up. I would spend our whole lives catching up.

Remember how we woke and the air was like mist? Like dreaming.

The next week was more of this new same. I skipped out on class each morning, though the week after, Don forced me to go, even gave me a ride on his way to work. But that first week was the bomb. I stayed home with you, Heather, curled up on the couch watching old DVDs of *Happy Days*. Your guilty pleasure, you told me.

"This is mostly what I do with my time these days," you said. You used to work, but when the rain came, even with all the jobs opening up, you couldn't bear to be out there in the world.

So, I did this with you, but on the last day of that first week, that Friday, I took your hand and led you to the door and slipped your steel boots onto your feet and my boots onto mine and we went outside and looked up at the gray sky. Your body shook. It hadn't rained all day, but the ground was still wet, and we stayed on the patio because you were too scared to slip into the grass.

"One time," you told me, "back in college, when I was your age, I had this boyfriend, right, and he drove me out to a field in the middle of nowhere. He had a bottle of wine, some fruity blackberry stuff, real cheap, but he'd forgot the corkscrew. I had a joint in my wallet, and we smoked that in the grass. Then we did it, nothing underneath us. Just lay right down in the grass and fucked. Afterward we threw the condom in this little stream. I always hoped some old farmer guy found it. That it made him think about what he was missing."

"I've never touched the grass," I said.

"Yeah, well," you said. "It's better that way."

"What does it feel like?"

"I don't know. Leathery. Slick, like. Green."

"I think I know," I said.

"Trust me, it's nothing special," you said. But I could tell you were lying. You'd loved the grass, the green, being part of it like that. You wrapped your arm around me and kissed the top of my head. You stopped shaking. I wondered what it was that had comforted you. Had you realized I could be taken care of? I always got the feeling that you just needed someone to take care of. Don was never that person. In that moment I decided I could be that person, at least for a little while. But I was a lot like you, and I needed someone to take care of for myself.

You know, I always wondered if I liked one of you better. I tried not to. I did my best to pay equal attention to you both. Now I have to admit, if I had to choose, I would've taken you in an instant. It was the way you looked at me. I could see that you needed it like no man could ever understand.

HUSBAND

Did my wife fall for you the way I fell for you? I don't think she did. In you I think we always saw what you were: a temporary person. We knew you would go, but she held on a little tighter, tried to swallow as much of you as she could before you went. She won't talk about you in the light, you know. When the sun's out, I can't even mention your name. We try to make it through the day without a reminder of you, but you've left all these artifacts around. I threw your toothbrush away, and the art book you gave her. When I walk down the hallway, past the painting Heather and I bought at an art auction when we were newly married, I remember that night we left the bed for a slice of toast and found you there before it, near to tears. It was an abstract piece, and we wondered what you could've seen in it to upset you.

"It's the brushstrokes," you told us. "It's about loss."

We stepped up close to it and studied the lines: jagged, spasmodic. Red and blue teardrop rain shapes and a thin line of green through the middle. Heather held you. I stood back and watched, knowing there was something there I couldn't touch.

Yes, my wife fell for you in some different way. When I saw her kiss you, saw her lips cross the pale hairs all over you, I caught my breath. There are some things about her I will never know. Moments and thoughts I can't touch. I'm aware that we do not think the same things when we fall into bed at night. I don't think about the roof over our heads, the thin line between us and the drip of burning water. I don't visualize water scarring my throat as I take a sip from the glass on the nightstand. Heather abandons so many glasses of water, uses them instead to water the potato plant she has begun to grow on our back patio, which she thinks I do not know about. I've seen her writing her letters to you, as I'm sure she's seen me writing mine. I'm aware that for each of these things that she does not know I know, there are more that will remain hidden from me.

Sometimes I'm glad you left. Always I wish we had never taken you home.

WIFE

It's redundant to say I miss you.

I wish you would come back to me.

I'm also weak sometimes. Because I remember you, I do. I lied.

Did you leave because of Don, because of the way he crossed his arms across his chest and scowled, because of the way things were just a little stiffer with him around, or was it because of the way he reacted when you began to disappear?

I know why you left. I'm not kidding myself. Maybe Don can pretend you're the bad guy, but I can't stomach the idea of hating you.

Your new woman can't love you like I love you.

LOVER

I know that year we had a routine. I know routine was something you guys clung to, something you made the defining factor of your life. I stayed over every night, after classes were through. I did homework while you, Don, made dinner. You were a great cook. Let me assure you, your cooking is not what chased me away. It was something indefinable. It was a chance at building something better, this competitiveness. I saw what you guys had, and I hated it, and I wanted more than anything to top it.

I broke routine. Instead of staying with you, I stayed home. You thought it began the first night I didn't show up, but it didn't. That night I was alone in my room with the quiet. It didn't rain, and for that I was grateful. I knew I would've panicked had it rained, wanted nothing more than to run to you, which of course I wouldn't have been able to.

But the sky was clear. I looked out my window and pretended I could see the stars you told me about.

The next day you guys asked me no questions. I told you nothing.

A week later I went to a party in the apartment across the way from mine instead of going to you. Some of my friends were there, happy to see me. It had been a while, since I was caught in the spell of you. They told me I looked older, darker. I felt funny when they said that, like that wasn't the way I was supposed to look. Having you should have made me brighter.

I stopped coming on the weekdays. Thursday nights I found fun, can you believe it, the kind of fun that seemed muted in your company. Not to say we never had it. But you guys were too serious, too often. I blame it on the rain, on having something and it being taken away. It was better never having it at all.

This is the best memory I have of you, of all my memories, maybe: we're in the kitchen, Heather, me and you. You're making dinner, a rare thing, Portobello mushroom sandwiches with creamed chipotle dressing. Gourmet olives from the Cook Islands. We both wished aloud we could live there, or on any of the other islands that had been repurposed, free of the rain we knew here. But they were, of course, closed to residents. We had lettuce too. It had been a long time since I'd had decent lettuce; the stuff in the dining hall at school, where I usually took my meals, was stringy, too green, artificial. This was real. I held the lettuce to my nose and took in the smell.

"What's it smell like?" you asked.

"Like nothing," I said. "A little like water, maybe. And green." I grinned.

"Oh? Like green, huh?" You reached over and grabbed it from me, tossed it onto the counter. Came at me with your palms bared.

I tried to run, but you were on me fast. Your hands wedged under my arms. You tickled me until I couldn't breathe.

"Truce!" I cried, and you fell for it.

After I took your breath in that other way, I ate the lettuce from the counter in one bite.

"Damn," I said. "That is fucking food."

Heather, your cheeks burned pink the whole night, and when Don came home, he thought you'd been drinking wine. But we hadn't been drinking at all. You had this smile stuck to your face, this hungry glow, like you could at any moment open your mouth and swallow the kitchen. Hell, swallow both of us. The world. The rain. That look on your face is how I want to remember you.

I hope I never see you again.

HUSBAND

We worried about you, you know. When the rain poured and you weren't in our bed, we worried if you were safe. We knew you'd taken to parties. We closed our eyes and prayed to no one that you were safe inside. I remembered what it was like, in college, how invincible you could feel. Back before the rain, it was easy for us to feel that way, even after college. We hoped you were smart about whatever you were doing.

I don't think we suspected that there was another man involved, at first. It didn't occur to me that you could want something other than the lavish life we gave you. After all, didn't you love the food? The films we found for you? Artist biopics from the 90's, the early 2000's? We knew you didn't have that where you went at night. We thought we were giving you all you ever wanted. I've said that before. I keep repeating myself because I don't understand.

Maybe I am, like Heather says, at a disadvantage, because I was never a young girl, and I was never someone who looked at paintings and saw the brushstrokes and knew the sorrow in them. I've never known much about sorrow. When the rain came, I saw the brightness; we'd had a long time, after all, to appreciate the way of the world before the rain. When bad things happen, I accept them and move on. I try to make the most of what I've been given. I've tried to make the most of you. I try to help her see things the way I do. Except regarding you, why you left. I let her think the man you left us for is a woman, despite what I know.

I'm not as dense as you think I am. I know that, being who I am, I can never understand her like you understand her. Because you could read her brushstrokes.

This is why I needed you. No other reason. And you gave me that, for a little bit. And I thank you. I wish this were easier to say.

WIFE

I knew about your new woman before you did, I think. When you first mentioned her name—your friend, Abigail—I knew in the way you said it. You said she was a new friend. Don never pieced it together. In fact, he still doesn't know. He thinks it was a man. He's sure it's a man. But I saw in the way you said it that she would be something to you. I know, too, when you found her, at one of those parties. I know how she got you, the way she carried herself. It was in the walk, wasn't it? She had the walk down, so sure. She had the voice, a little gruff, and that way of saying your name: as if it were a piece of art.

I like to think I said your name like that.

But let me be clear, I don't blame you. You saw a chance at your own thing, and you took it. Part of me hopes you're happy. The other part hopes she'll break your naïve heart.

All of me wishes, every day you're gone, that you'll come back.

Listen to this; I'm a broken record of broken heart clichés. It makes me sick how average you were. How ordinary. How you could have been any woman, anywhere. But you were you. And that makes the difference.

The day I knew you'd chosen was during the week right after my birthday, when we were supposed to meet up at the house, then go out for a change, anywhere, maybe to the coffee shop, maybe to the market to pick up the supplies for dinner. I wanted to go out for you. We could make food together; I always wanted to repeat that memory. But you didn't show up.

I stood at the window. The rain began. I watched it fall. The sun went down. The hour when Don usually got back came closer. I was glad he'd be home soon.

I wished the damn rain would stop. If it would just stop, I would find you. I would go into the cold for you. I wanted to hold you. I want to hold you. We both want to hold you again.

LOVER

His name was Clark. I think his parents named him after Superman, but he was the skinniest dude I'd ever seen. So skinny I didn't mind when he pressed his weight on top of me. I liked it, even. We didn't meet at a party, and he wasn't the love of my life, but he was something of my very own and I had to have him. He was often sad, and I could kiss him and make it okay for a little while. There are these little moments of knowing what one wants, and if you don't grab them they just go away.

I'll spare you the details. But know that he was special to me and not special. Know that you were, too.

Don't worry, Don. I'm not going to tell her. I'll keep our secret.

HUSBAND

I'm sorry. I have to say it, while I can. Maybe it's why I'm really writing this. For what I did to you, I'm sorry.

The truth is I was shocked to see you again. You didn't text, didn't call. You just showed up at the door. I opened it and saw you and that grey sky above you, and I wanted to let you in, but Heather was asleep. You going, you see, it did something to us and for us. When you stopped returning our calls, we wrapped our arms around each other, and she cried into her pillow. I cried a little, too. You meant more to us than we let on to one another, and to realize that we had held these similar feelings buried when we should have shared them, it meant something. In losing you, we were bonded in our grief. So when you showed up at our door that day, I didn't let you in.

"It's him," you said. "I don't know why he did it."

Your face was streaked with red.

"Him?" I asked.

"You know. It was too fast. To see his fucking skin like that."

"This is the guy?"

"His skin. I've never seen anything like it. It just … the smell."

Like burnt rubber. I remembered. I had seen my share. We didn't know better back then. "It's a hard thing to see," I said.

"Please, can I come in?"

"No."

"Please? She'll want to see me. If she knew I was out here …."

"You can't come in." I stepped out and shut the door behind me. "What you did to us, of course you can't come in. We can't take care of you anymore. You made a choice. It's too hard to go back once you've left."

"He died," you said. I hated the word. I knew you were thinking on it too, how short, how harsh a word. "It fucked him up, and he—"

"You need to go home." I pointed up. "It's going to start again. Soon. Go home, take care of yourself."

I kissed you, a cruel thing. You tasted like salt, whiskey.

"Please don't tell her you were here," I said. "It'll hurt her."

You didn't respond, just got in your car and drove.

I'm sorry I did that to you, but you have to understand. When things are over, they're over, and there can be no turning back. I found the conclusion I was looking for, and you were asking for a different end.

WIFE

I've lied to you a little. It's not all bad since you left. When I'm with him, I feel like I maybe do love him like the day we met. I think what I loved in you was an idea. I think you might have healed something in us I didn't think could be fixed. I sing in the shower now, and when I emerge from the bathroom steam I wrap myself in a towel and sit before the window and watch the rain drip down the glass, leaving trails down the RainAway chemical window treatment like the snails used to leave down the sticky leaves of my zucchini plants. These days I don't cry for you or for him. I cry because it empties me of the salt that once dried me up, because I've lost something I've held onto most of my life: the sadness, my old friend. I keep potatoes again, though they are genetically altered, the dirt synthetic. I feed them with bottled water. Don and I have even begun to open up to each other, admitting all the secrets we've kept from one another. I told him about the time we made cupcakes but ate them before he got home. Also the time we did it on his desk.

Still, I'll ask you one more time: come back to me.

There. It's over. That's all I'll say.

I'll leave you with a memory. We were all three together, one of those first weeks. You asked how we met.

"At a party," I said. "He had the walk."

"And she had the beer." Don laughed. He used to laugh a lot, less so in recent years, and that moment I realized he was, in many ways, the man I married still. We never had children, and we didn't want you for that, but we wanted you to complete us.

It was too much to ask of a young woman. I will ask no more of you, except this: be sure, when someone in your future asks how you and your woman met, that the answer doesn't shame you.

LOVER

This piece is hers; if you ever want me, ever in your whole long life, I'm still yours. No guarantee on how long I'll last, but I will come to you.

This, his; take her outside, to a field of grass you can touch—find it wherever you can, if it takes the whole of your life, and let her bathe in the green.

You were familiar to me. Not as familiar as the town I grew up in; no one could ever be that familiar. But I smelled and saw you everywhere. You had a bowl cut like the Beatles. It made me laugh. You were not attractive until I saw you up close.

I came home one night from a party, my breath whiskey-soaked. You were sitting on my couch like you belonged there.

"What are you doing here?" I asked, wobbling, holding my key out at you like a weapon.

Andrew stood in the doorway. He sniffed twice at the air. "Calm, Nora, this is Grayson," he said. "He works with me at the warehouse."

Of course, I thought. My roommate knew everyone. He was always bringing people back to our house. I knew then what kind of person you might be. You didn't have a lot of friends. Why else would you be here with him? You were awkward and adverse to authority. Otherwise, Andrew's conspiracy theories would have scared you away. You didn't do your homework or go to class, or else you wouldn't be in a stranger's house on a Wednesday night. You smelled like the woods far, far away from this town, farther away even than the town where Andrew and I grew up.

"Want to smoke a joint with us?" Andrew asked. You still said nothing. I wondered if you could talk. I'd never seen you smile.

"No," I said, walking past you to my room.

THE TOWN I CAME FROM is called Agape. The name means love without body. The name means love without sex. No one leaves Agape.

No one but Andrew and me.

THE FIRST DREAMS I HAD about you were nightmares. You were standing in my doorway as I slept. I woke and bolted from bed. I made sure the door was locked. I could hear laughter and the rip of bong water from the living room.

In the morning, you were passed out on our couch. The blanket had slid down your chest, and I could see your flabby stomach, pasty white as the moon. My stomach growled. I grabbed a white bread bagel on my way out the door. I never skipped class. I never got hangovers. Not from drinking, not from drugs. I walked to class with your blank gaze burning behind my eyes.

The second dreams I had about you were sweaty. I woke to slick sheets. I woke to blood and cramps. I woke to tingling skin and the deep belly urge to plunge my fingers between my legs until my breath came out hard and quick as a chased predator's. Your skin, in those dreams, tasted like sunlight and honey. You were always naked.

The next time I saw you, sitting on a bench outside the history building, you smiled at me. Your smile was as ugly and crooked as death. No wonder you rarely smiled. Your smell was overwhelming, then, like the scent of a home I'd never realized that I had. I knew with a gut animal instinct that you were not who I had thought you were. I was willing to give you a try.

IN AGAPE, THE PEOPLE STARVE themselves, of food, of blood, of water, of rosy cheeks and sex; they go to school and church and then to their houses where they lock themselves in and try to ignore the howls in their own throats. In Agape, a group of high school friends used to sneak out and lose themselves to the moon every month. There was the wind against our skin as we ran through streets empty of life. There were the bones we buried in our parents' backyards. Small towns are full of secrets.

THE VODKA SLID DOWN OUR throats like water. I was parched. The moon was full. Without liquor, I grew restless. Every night, caged in my room. The vodka set me free. So did your smell, of that other place I wanted so badly to see. But I never thought you could last, even though I suspected you might be more than met my eye. Men never lasted long.

We did not sleep together then. You were my roommate's friend, and his scent was all over you, too, like cologne. Instead, I took home other men, made rough love to them with my eyes shut tight. I pretended they were you. Still, you went with me to bars, to parties I sniffed out. We walked down streets until we heard laughter, until we sniffed the skunk smell of dank weed. At parties, we stuck side by side at first, until the moon trembled tentatively in the sky and it was time to pick a partner and go home.

Each night, I hugged you goodbye so close I could smell your sweat stink. I let it rub off onto my shirt. When I fucked those other people, I left my shirt on. I let them go in the mornings with bite marks across their necks.

Sometimes, you were on the couch, pretending to sleep. Once, when I asked why you had come there, you said Andrew asked you over. Sometimes, Andrew went to the party with us. But always you clung to him as though he was the leader of your pack. I came to know the reason; you wanted to be close enough to protect me, if I needed it. I never needed it. You could hear the gasp screams that came from my room. I imagine that to you they were a sick lullaby.

I was not good to you. I don't know why you stomached it.

IN AGAPE, THERE WERE TWO boys and three girls who ran their claws down each other's bodies and made moan noises to match the coyote howls. There were hideaways in the hills. There was a playground with a plastic slide where I had my first boy. There was a taste of his lips like rotten meat in my mouth, happily never after. There were five kids who just wanted to fill themselves to the brim with whatever food they could find: muscle and fat and skin like jerky. There were kids who did what they could to survive in a town with no life to it.

I GO BACK AND FORTH. I should have let it simmer longer, the lust. I should have taken you sooner. I should have left you alone. I should have taken you and you only. But it was good when we finally fucked. You would hate it if you heard me call it that. You had a gentle way of saying things. I loved to watch you blush.

We went camping, all of the pack. Me and you and Andrew and the temporary people who floated in and out of our lives like specks in the corners of our eyes. In a college town, that was bound to happen, people still getting to know themselves. Very few people liked me once they got to know me—too predatory and wild and ambitious. You, though. You stuck around and made friends of an enemy.

I insisted on us having our own private tent together. We swallowed three grams of 'shrooms and went walking. The river was a snake. The water was your spilled blood. Not yet, I said. You thought I meant sex. I meant death. I took you by the river. You were soft and sweet and your skin hummed and shifted. In the dark, you looked familiar, like your old town might have been like ours, like you might be like us.

"Are you one of us?" I asked.

"I'm one with you," you said.

It wasn't what I meant. We zipped the tent and unzipped our pants and unzipped our skins and knew each other bone by bone.

"Not yet," I whispered.

When you came, you howled like a dying dog.

"This is where you came from," you said. "This is who you are."

In Agape, I drove you around the city on the main street which wrapped like teeth around the fire station, past the lone cop car that sat empty in the church parking lot, past the BBQ joint with the smell of roasting flesh, past the house I had been raised in.

"Can we go in?" you asked.

"No."

"It's so quiet," you said. "There's no one. Is anyone home?"

"They're home. They're hiding. They all hide, here."

I kept on driving. The streets were as dead as the day I had left them.

We shared shots of vodka like it would make us drink less. You told me I needed to drink less. I told you to shut your mouth and kissed you. I bit you so your lips bled. You liked it. But we had become used to each other, used to the noises we made when in heat. I knew every scratch on you. You knew my scars from those Agape days. Boredom makes even a feast taste like ash on the tongue.

"Take me anywhere," you said. "We need to get away for a while."

I wanted you to drive. I wanted to see where you came from. But you shook your head. "Too tired," you said. "Too tired to drive."

There was only one place where I knew the way.

In Agape, there is a sign. Welcome, it reads.

"Do you feel welcome?" I asked you.

You looked over at me. Already, I was forgetting everything I had learned since leaving. In Agape I am the same stupid teenager I was in high school. In Agape, I am as hungry as a growing girl. My stomach growled. You were kind enough not to mention it. But you had a look in your eye; you were wary of me. You saw that my pupils were dilating, that my eyes were darkening. You saw that I was who I had always been.

"No," you said. "I don't know you here."

We came to the playground behind the church. I wanted to show you the spot where it had all begun, where I had first bled for a boy. I would bleed for you, I wanted to say. I should have bled for you. But you weren't one of us after all.

Some things never change. You smelled like the first time. You bled like the most intoxicating liquor I had ever tasted. You did not bite back.

Now I GATHER YOUR BONES and the bloody shroud of your skin and drive home. Out of Agape, back to the house I share with Andrew.

"Where's Grayson?" he asks, but he doesn't expect an answer. He knows without looking at me. He has always known. We are two of a pack.

Together we bury your bones in our back yard. We build a garden over them.

Some nights I still dream about you. I wake up with your taste on my tongue. Times like these, I go out to the garden and pick red tomatoes from the stalk. I sink my teeth into them. Juice drips all over my hands, my feet, my thighs. I imagine that you are here with me. That you are the pulsing moon. That you are in Agape, waiting for me to retrieve you, to save you, to carry you home.

THE MAMMOTH SKELETON STANDS IN the distance, barely visible below the drooping limbs of monstrous evergreens. My father and I have been watching it now for an hour from our campsite, seated comfortably in blue nylon chairs. The mammoth is scavenging, and with our binoculars, we've seen it pull leaf after leaf from the smaller oaks. The leaves collect in its mouth of solid bone. Earlier, it tried to swallow one, but the leaf passed down the throat into the ribcage and then fell from between the narrow bones. The mammoth stomped, crushing the leaves into dust. It hasn't swallowed one since.

"It must be a mother mammoth," I say.

"No way," Dad says. "It's a daddy. Look at its tusks. Too big for a female."

"Yeah, okay." I put down the binoculars. "Clearly a male, a papa mammoth, sure."

My father has this hope in his eyes, gazing at that

mammoth, and it kills me. Makes my stomach flop. He's always been a wishful thinker, ever since I was a little girl. I'm as old as he was when he and Mom had me, but that silly hopefulness hasn't disappeared.

What I want to say to my father is, grow up. Quit living in the past. You're only a small part of this world now. But I could never say this. Despite his obsoleteness, I love him with this outdated kind of love. The emotion even feels dusty in my chest, like it's something I should cough out.

From the ice chest, I take the jar of mayo and the bread and the turkey. I make two sandwiches and eat mine as he *oohs* and *aahs* at the mammoth skeleton. Mammoths, I've seen before. What I'm hoping for is a bald eagle skeleton, or maybe even a giant sea turtle skeleton in the lake—they're hard to find. Skittish. Plus, there are so few in this part of the world. Most of them inhabit the coasts, bury themselves in the black oceans. I know this not because I've been to the ocean, but because my father has told me. He's full of knowledge like that, which is why I don't argue about the mammoth being a father. His hopefulness doesn't force him to lie; rather he seeks out instances of himself in nature, in daily life, clings to ancient movies. Father of the Bride is his favorite. When he watches it, I pretend I don't know the glisten in his eyes is there because he likely won't see me down an aisle.

The mammoth moves on, the leaves still collected in its mouth, its huge metacarpals thumping the ground, and even at our campsite, we feel the vibrations under our feet.

Dad taps me on the shoulder, urgent. He hasn't looked away from the mammoth skeleton, with the binoculars glued to his face like a second pair of eyes.

"He's going, he's going," he says. "Look, Maya, look."

I raise the binoculars. "Guess he's going home."

Part of me wishes we could do the same. Only I don't want to go back to my drafty apartment or Dad's empty shack of a house. I want to go back to the house I grew up in, to our family. With Mom around, Dad had a purpose, someone he could make laugh. He was less obsolete, less a relic from a distant age before the virus attacked any human with a Y chromosome. There were few survivors; my dad was one of them. Maybe the world still had a use for him, I don't know. Maybe he was just one of the lucky ones.

So, things change. People die. Whole species die off, then the remaining endangered fade until they are nothing but bone. They haven't fixed death the way they've fixed conception, which they were forced by circumstance to do. Even if we went back to our old house, it would be smaller than I remember.

The mammoth disappears. After about ten minutes, Dad lowers his binoculars. His smile is gone.

"I made you a sandwich," I say.

EARLY IN THE MORNING, I bolt to the underbrush by the restrooms and vomit. Yesterday, I was able to hide my sickness from Dad, but this morning was a close call. I'm almost sure he can hear it. If he asks, I'll tell him I ate a bad apple before bed.

I can't tell him the truth, yet. It'll break him. He wants so badly for me to cling, like he does, to the past.

I wipe my mouth and pat my belly on top of my shirt. You bastard, I say. See what I'm dealing with for you?

I don't feel anything under there. It's too early.

When I get back to the campsite, Dad's still asleep. His snores carry from the tent. I crawl back in my bag and pretend I never left.

I SMELL SAUSAGE. CLIMBING FROM the tent, I hear its sizzle. This trip must've taken all year to save for. I tried to pay for it, but he wouldn't let me. He never lets me pay.

"You shouldn't have spent so much," I say.

He holds his finger to his lips. Points out into the woods. When I squint, I'm able to make out the faint form of a deer, a real flesh deer, frozen in its tracks, its eyes glinting in the light that reaches through the trees.

"Another daddy?" I whisper.

"Don't be silly," he says. "It's obviously a baby."

I take a seat at the worn, moldy picnic table. The bench creaks, and I feel fat already. But I know I'm not even showing yet. On the tabletop sits an empty wooden pipe and a lighter. Guess Dad's been up a while.

Dad scoops some sausage onto my plate. I'm starving, so I pick the patties up with my hands and shovel them into my mouth.

"Geez, girl. Haven't seen you eat like that since you were a teenager."

Dad takes smaller bites, plops a couple of patties from his plate onto mine. "My appetite's not all it used to be."

When we used to go camping, Dad and I would bring along whole rolls of chocolate chip cookie dough and eat it straight from the tube until we felt sick. We would eat breakfast burritos with egg and cheese and sausage and fresh tomatoes. Skillet apple cobbler. Trail mix with cashews and marshmallows singed over the fire. Mom used to buy so much food for us we would've been set even if we were stranded for weeks. With Dad's modest income from warehouse work and the occasional sperm bank donation—every remaining man's duty—there is just enough for breakfast, lunch, and dinner, though it seems as though he's purchased only luxuries for those three meals. I've snuck along trail mix and a roll of cookie dough. A surprise.

"I thought we'd go down to the lake today. See if we can't spot that mammoth again." Dad rinses both our plates with water from a jug, stows them back in our bag which we'll leave in the car on the way out so that the bears—flesh-and-fur bears—don't get it.

I grab my swimsuit and a bag and a piece of ginger root I've brought to nibble on. A friend of mine tells me it will help with the sickness. At this point I'll try anything.

●●

GOOD MEN ARE IMPOSSIBLE TO find, so I stopped searching. For every twenty women these days, there's one man, and I didn't have the patience to deal with them. It's like getting used to being treated as a rarity, being seen as something special, has made them too big-headed and lazy to do anything on their own.

Dating isn't for me. Some girls still dig it, sure, but usually those are the girls so tightly wound by work or kids that they just need some kind of release. It's like a competition. The problem is it's uneven. The women have all the cards: the money, the careers, the children. What do men have, now that they're coddled by their meager government pensions? Penises. Given, they can feel good, great even; but the packages that come with them are too often damaged.

I tried. Not long, but I tried. Even tried a few women, but I couldn't make myself desire them like I did men. Turns out Dad's the last good man on Earth, and even he gets that weak look in his eye sometimes, which he never used to get when Mom was alive. I just couldn't hunt around anymore, and I know Dad always thought I shared his and Mom's values, but he hasn't been out there in the modern world as much as I have. He hides away in his shack and reads about stars and skeletons.

The clinic I went to for the insemination had metal chairs and cream-colored walls, a big fish tank with several species of skeleton fish. I tried not to watch them, because each time I did I thought how Dad would look if he saw me here. I'd picked a place far from the donation center, so the chances of him walking by and seeing me in the window would be slight.

They called me into the back. A nurse led me down a hall, took my weight, height, blood pressure. Sat with me in the room and went over my paperwork. It was easy. With me right at the proper age, a healthy income, steady background.

They handed me the tablet with the file I had chosen from their online database. Handsome guy, black silk for hair, dark eyes. A natural sample, not one they'd altered but rather one from the old days, frozen all this time. The guy was an artist, classical-looking stuff—he'd submitted a picture of his, a portrait of a woman. I could tell he had loved her. It was why I picked him. The capacity for romantic love, maybe it was genetic. Maybe I'd missed out on it, like it was recessive or something and got buried in me.

I signed the form saying that yes, he was the one. Yes, I understood that the procedure could, in rare cases, result in twins or triplets or sextuplets, or that there was another small chance it wouldn't take; they'd figured out the perfect timing, the amount to use, all that, long ago. Feet in the stirrups, I gripped the arm of the chair hard. The speculum cold inside me, the tube of warm sample stiff. The cramps seized me, and I clasped my hands together and squeezed.

The old way, at least, probably felt better.

AT THE LAKE, I READ while Dad swims. He ducks under the surface and stays too long. When he comes up, his goggles are filled with water. He must've stayed down there watching for skeletons until the water came up past his vision.

"Anything good?" I call out.

"Absolutely," he says. "Come on in."

The book I'm reading, an anthology of men's fiction, isn't that great. I'd much rather be reading the baby books I snuck along. For a moment I think of pulling one out, getting it over with. Instead, I toss the anthology into the dirt and run down into the lake so I get used to it all at once.

"Check this out." He hands me the goggles. "A lone whiskerfish. Probably separated from its—"

"Family?"

Dad smiles. He has a warm smile. "School. From its school."

Underwater the upkicked dirt hazes my view, but through a very small window I glimpse the flicker of a tailbone. A huge shadow passes over my head. Bubbles swirl out from the force of its movement. I look up. The skinny lizard-shaped underskeleton of a sea turtle, the shell large as a television screen, treads the lake fog with its phalanges. It paddles away.

"Did you see that?" I ask once I'm up again, ripping the goggles off and handing them over.

My father goes under. Comes up. Shakes his head.

"Sea turtle," I say. "Right above my head."

This time my father's smile is colder, stretched a little too tight. I imagine for a moment I can see his jawbone behind that smile. I shiver. "Sorry I missed it," he says. "But what a sight for you. You'll probably remember it the rest of your life. You'll tell this story to your own family. Likely the last one this half of the country." He squeezes my shoulder with his big, red hands. I want to tell him he'll see one, one of these days. But this was probably his last chance.

OVER THE COURSE OF THE years, we've seen the following skeletons: snow leopard, whiskerfish, mammoths, jackrabbits, countless birds darting around on skeleton wings, bull trout, baby stegosauruses, and even a couple of bearcats. Dad's right. Someday, I'll tell my family about the sea turtle, even if it isn't the kind of family he envisions for me.

Night falls, and the stars glow. The one thing that's never changed about these trips is the stars. Out comes Dad's portable telescope, and he assembles it atop the picnic table. I fix us some crackers and bring out the cookie dough, offer him a pinch once his hands are free.

"What a daughter," he says, mouth full. "Too bad your Mom can't be here."

"Mom never came with us," I say.

"She'd be so proud of you." He peers into the scope.

"Because I brought cookie dough?"

"Check out the moon," he says.

The moon is low and round and beautiful, and impossible to see from the city. "Gorgeous," I say, because I understand that often my father needs encouragement. And it is gorgeous.

In the dark, I hear the flick of a lighter. The bright of the flame floods the air with light pollution. Dad always said it takes at least thirty minutes to become readjusted to the dark. I look over at Dad, pipe to his lips.

"Smoke a little doobavitch?" he says.

I always have before. It's been one of the things that cemented our bond, once I was old enough.

"No thanks," I say. I open my mouth, close it, open it again. "I'm, uh, my throat's been itchy all week."

The air now is smoky, the skunk smell overwhelming. It enters through my nose and collects in my throat, my stomach it feels like; as if I've swallowed smoke, and of course the smell rises up, up. I run to the bushes on the other side of the table, hand cupped over my mouth, and puke crackers and cookie dough.

Dad's hand is on my shoulder. "You okay?"

"Fine." I stand. He hands me his towel from earlier. "Guess I am getting sick."

"Do you wanna go home? I could drive you, come back tomorrow and pack up."

"I'll be okay," I say. "I just need some sleep."

Outside the tent I hear Dad smoking and coughing for another hour or so. I think about that moment in the lake when I thought I could see his skeleton showing through. It makes me shiver again. I have to tell him. He has a right to know he'll be a grandfather.

The door zips open. The ground rattles under Dad's big feet as he clomps into the tent. His sleeping bag is in the other half, and we're facing opposite ways so our feet end up right next to one another in the middle. I hear him settle into his bag and sigh his pre-sleep sigh.

"It's amazing the stars haven't changed much since even I was a boy," he says.

"I'm pregnant," I say, before I lose the nerve.

There's a tense silence for a moment, as if he isn't sure he heard me right.

"Well, great," he says. "When will I meet him?"

He means the father. I'm tempted to pretend I think he means the child, but Dad deserves better.

"You won't," I say. "He died a long time ago, fifty years or so."

Another silence, this one worse, this one less a product of confusion, more a product of disbelief.

"I went to a clinic, Dad."

"I know. I'm not a moron."

"I don't think you are. I had to. I want a child. I tried to find someone, to do it your way, but—"

"Your life, Maya."

The finality in his voice would be impossible to crack. I say nothing more. I let my body take over. It pushes me into a troubled sleep.

THE NEXT DAY, DAD'S GOT bags under his eyes. He looks older, skin thinner and ashen, stretched tight without the smile, so tight his wrinkles have become deep creases in his cheeks. Shadows float in the sky. Later, it'll rain. He slides my plate over to me without a word, and we say nothing as we eat. The rest of the day, I know, will be much the same.

While I'm sitting at the table, looking out into the thicket of trees across the way—Dad's right, this place is beautiful—Dad gets up and grabs his jacket and heads off down the trail to the restroom. Thirty minutes pass before I realize he isn't coming back. I trudge down the path, knock on the restroom door. When there's no answer, I open it. Empty. I continue down the path.

Above me a woodpecker—flesh and blood, they're still alive and thriving, like the bears—stabs away at a tree. I pass the river, the water grey and deep, cold if I were to touch it. The wind picks up, rattles branches. I crunch rocks underfoot. I wish Dad were with me to point out what trees are what, which clouds mean it will rain, and when we should head back to the campsite.

I'm so absorbed in watching that I don't see the distant figure before me, massive in the trees. The mammoth skeleton's femurs jut and retract as it inches forward, skull turning from side to side on its axis. I wonder if it misses its fur. Trying to make as little sound as possible, I follow.

It leads me through brush, across a gravel path, and back into the trees. Lucky for me that it moves so slow. My muscles are working overtime. Vines cut at my legs through my jeans, snag and slow me down. My t-shirt rips at the bottom hem. I stop. The mammoth doesn't seem to hear.

It's then, paused, listening to make sure the mammoth doesn't know I'm there, I hear this sound coming from it, a murmur like bones rattling and scraping together. I've heard rumor of talking skeletons, but never have I heard one before. My breath catches. I don't know that it's speaking any language I can understand, but the idea of such a tremendous beast with words stuns me; what secrets he must have, what things he must have seen.

It takes another few steps. I follow, and we're in a clearing. I don't go all the way in, but peering through the leaves I see the mammoth go to the far brush and emit this blood-curdling screech like a nail on a chalkboard, and from the brush crawls another large one, the mother I guess, who nuzzles her skull against the first's, and then a little one bounds out and stops under its parents, pushes against their leg bones. The father opens his jaw and lets a pile of leaves fall. The child scrambles for them, but when it swallows, just like before, the leaves fall through the bones of its ribcage. It tries again and again, and I notice then that the ground is covered in crumbled leaves. I wish again that my father were here to see this.

I turn and try to run, but my energy's drained, my muscles pounding, and the brush too thick to move quickly. I'm forced to amble back to camp, stopping often to catch breaths. I memorize the landmarks so I can bring Dad back. I'll bet he went looking for them, too, and returned to camp when he failed.

Once camp's in sight, I force myself to run. Outside the tent, I stop, hold my belly, feel a little like puking, but it passes. I've never been all that athletic. A shadow moves in the tent.

"I saw the mammoth family," I call out. "You were right." Next to the tent, I smell that rain musk gathering in the air, mixed with the nylon of the tent, the plastic of the zipper. "I'm coming in, Dad, better be dressed." I feel like bouncing up and down, as if I were ten years old again.

I crawl through the opening, shoes on. I'll get in trouble, I think, smiling to myself, dirty up the tent. I straighten and look at my father.

He's dressed, but the parts of his skin I can see are halfway gone, the skeleton showing through the outer parts of his cheeks, his arms, his hands which he now holds in front of his face as if he's playing peek-a-boo with me.

"Don't," he says. "Don't look at me."

I reach forward and push his hands away. I can't help but stare at him. His lips curl back so his teeth show through in a grotesque smile. His big toe's still pink with skin, but the rest have turned to pure bone. I can see the bones connected to one another by nothing but air, the skin of his forehead, his wrists, his nose like patches sewed on sloppily so they hang loose, curled like wet pages at the edges.

"Oh, Dad," I say. There is no light in the tent, and his form is shadowy, dark.

"Dad." I say again. "I'm sorry, Dad."

The first drops of rain patter atop the tent. I wrap my arms around him and hug him hard. The bones shift and creak under the weight of my embrace.

"Me, too," he says. His voice husky. "I'm sorry, too. Your child," he says.

I burrow my head into the crook of his neck. I'll tell him all about his grandpa, I think, but I can't tell Dad this, can't suggest out loud he won't be there to see the baby's first breath. I squeeze until I feel him crack beneath me, until the bones groan like an antique house. I feel them slipping apart, feel his skin sliding off, but I can't let go. I won't. I hear something fall into the dirt, but I don't look to see. I'll keep holding onto him. I'll keep holding on until there's nothing left.

well.

also, something about that skeleton analogy?

TORI TAKES ANOTHER HIT OF Nostalgia. The smoke is creamy mint cookie down her throat, smooth and hot. It fills her lungs, tickles, burns, and as she coughs it out, she laughs, smoke pouring from her lips. Fog fills her head. The live oaks' winter skeletons crisp into focus as the drug takes hold. Tori feels the cold on her skin as if she is a little girl in the snow, her hand in her father's glove, surrounded by his smell of smoke and vodka. Her mother hates the cold but watches from the window. Tori's belly is full. It hasn't been this full for years, not since home, that word a lighthouse beacon she will never again reach without this burn of throat, cloud of mind, her parents having pushed her out once they met her first girlfriend. Tori passes the pipe to her companion.

"I haven't done Nostalgia in years," Kay says. "Since I was in college. Homesick."

"No pressure," Tori says. "Just offering."

Her new friend confuses her; she's never been with a slate before, and even though Kay is pre-op, it's taken some concentration not to mix up the pronouns. Shu, Tori practices on nights that Kay does not sleep over. Shur. Still, she's messed up a couple of times, accidentally said she instead of shu, her instead of shur.

Kay flicks the lighter over the blue-black herb but does not inhale. Instead, shu watches the leaves char in the pipe's bowl.

"Hey, knock it off." Tori grabs the pipe, the lighter. "Don't waste it."

"Sorry." Kay shrugs shur thick shoulders. The grey scarf around shur neck shifts in the breeze. Tori itches to bat the decorative balls which hang from it but doesn't.

Instead, she remembers. When she was a little girl, she had an orange cat who batted at her scarves. Another cat in college, living with that first girlfriend, Meredith. Meredith's skin against her own, protection from the cold, a laugh like medicine she didn't know she needed.

"You okay?" Kay asks, squeezing the nub of her shoulder. Tori opens her eyes. She had closed them without realizing. This is sad to her, like the day Meredith moved up north.

"Fine," she says. "Cold is all."

Later, atop the flannel red-and-white holiday sheets, Tori closes her eyes again and imagines familiar fingers, longer and thinner than Kay's, inside her, lets the Nostalgia hum within like a tongue, lets herself dissolve into the memory of love. One day, she thinks, kissing the nape of Kay's bare neck, shu will feel like memory, shur blank, nippleless chest a comfort of familiarity rather than this stiff newness, this gloss. Tori wants it dull like a pencil worn to the nub.

When they are finished, breathless in one another's embrace, Tori burrows her face in the hair of Kay's armpits, the smell of animal musk and orgasm. As the Nostalgia wears off, a veil lifts on this moment, the past fogging instead like a breathed-upon window. Kay's skin is real under her ear, the drum of shur heartbeat a surge through her. It makes her own heart beat faster, her palms sweat. She swallows her spit. To quiet the silence, she pulls her face from the sweat of Kay's body and examines shur in the room's dark.

"Your photographs," she says, "they're good."

Kay laughs. "I know. Is that the only reason you're with me?"

Tori lets her head fall back into place. She knows that Kay is not comfortable enough yet to push, and the question is difficult to answer. Yes, she should say, the photographs. But this would be too much. It would stress her throat, already sore from the smoke. Behind her eyes, she recalls the photographs, dancers leaping from frame to frame like in a flip book.

Tori had glimpsed Kay every day at the college as Kay walked past Tori mopping the same spot again and again, trying to look busy so that she would not have to catch Kay's eye. Because she knew who Kay was, had seen shur picture in the school paper, had heard shur name repeated back when Tori was a student, back before her only affiliations with the school were the mop and broom they issued her, the paycheck they sent her monthly for cleaning the classrooms and bathrooms of the art buildings.

Whenever Tori had a moment, she stopped to stare at Kay's photographs. Once she dared to touch them; she wanted to see if the dancer was real, some little person imprisoned in the film, forced to tango and ballet and flamenco hour after hour, day after day, year after year, but it was just paper under Tori's finger, glossy as what would be Tori and Kay's future bedroom shenanigans. The dancers were always slates, or disguised as slates. Tori couldn't believe there could be so many of them in Riddle, Texas, their small college town. And the way they changed from photo to photo, like devils. Like angels. Like monsters. Like memories Tori struggled to remember without the help of smoke down her throat.

"Do you want to learn how to take them?" Kay asks. "I can teach you. I think you'd be good at it."

The idea sends a shiver down Tori's spine; it both intrigues and terrifies her. Too new.

"I can't," she says.

Tori is at the sink filling a glass with water when Meredith knocks at the kitchen door.

"Whose car is that outside?" Meredith asks as she pushes past Tori. "You better not dance for her, whoever she is." In the time since she has been away, she's shaved the sides of her head so that the middle patch of hair falls over two bald spots. "If you dance for her, I swear."

It isn't a surprise to see Meredith there, but also it is a surprise, as each time she shows up, it sends a shock down Tori's belly to her groin. A Pavlov's bell. Tori leaves the faucet on, lets the water run over the sides of the glass and down the drain.

"I don't dance," Tori says, leaning against the sink, digging her hands into the pockets of her pajama pants.

"Bullshit you don't dance," Meredith says. "We used to dance all the time."

"Not anymore. I only danced with you."

Meredith's smile dimples her cheeks. She looks stronger, thicker; from her letters, Tori knows that she's been climbing rocks, running races, cycling across mountains until her muscles quiver. "Prove it," she says.

Even though Kay is in the other room, asleep with shur head on Tori's pillow, Tori's belly aches for a kiss she knows the taste of. Berries and salt. If she could bury her head in Meredith's hair, she would smell the slick oil sweet. She knows this. She knows, too, the way Meredith will move against her in a dance of sweat, the way Meredith will not let Tori touch her. The way she will, once Tori is gasping in her arms, jump up and disappear to the bathroom, how she will emerge flushed and breathless. How she will say, "I took care of it myself." And how Tori will accept this. She knows, too, that as they sit on the couch with their legs intertwined, Meredith will not ask about Kay.

Sure enough, it happens like that. Meredith is out the door twenty minutes later. When Tori crawls back into bed, Kay rolls over and kisses the top of her forehead.

"I don't care, you know, about her," Kay says. "I think you'll find I'm pretty open-minded."

"I don't know what you're talking about." Tori closes her eyes and counts the hours until she can light up again.

WHEN SHE RUNS OUT OF Nostalgia, she calls up her high school friend, Logan. He and her other friends from that time have never left the small town where they all grew up together, Agape, where they spent weekends downing stolen vodka and imbibing a rainbow assortment of drugs until Nostalgia became their drug of choice.

One hour's drive south and Tori is knocking on Logan's door. Logan answers, his skintight jeans smeared with forgotten food particles. His eyes are red as emergency exit letters. When he wraps his arms around her, she feels as though this moment has already occurred. Déjà vu. Of course, it's happened once every two weeks for the last six years of her life.

"You have some?" she asks.

Logan leads her by the hand back to his room, where four old friends and one man Tori has never seen sit around a hookah. Inside his parents' house, everything is the same: the black curtains drawn across every window, the stuffed moose head mounted above the neglected fireplace, the smell of stale smoke and semen-filled napkins left too long in Logan's wastebasket. The coal atop the hookah smolders redder than their eyes. As Tori's eyes adjust, her chest constricts; it's a scene straight from senior year when she didn't yet know who she was, when she hadn't yet grown into her own skin, was still shy and ashamed of herself, awkward in her body. This is a thought she struggles to swallow every time she comes here. Instead, she takes the pipe they pass her and sucks in the rancid smoke. Once her eyes match theirs, she feels right again. She looks from face to face in the circle.

Back in the day, they used to sneak into the woods to smoke this stuff. They broke into a rundown shed and sat on a ratty couch that smelled of mildew. They nearly got caught by the cops a couple of times, but they were young. Maybe that is the difference, Tori thinks, *I know now that I can crumble like charred Nostalgia.* There was another one of them back then, a boy Tori thought for a while that she loved. They let Daniel be their leader, clung to his every word. She let him be her first boy—the only mistake she ever admitted to. She recalled his lips on her neck, his fingers tracing the necklace he slipped around her neck like a collar. *This is not the way,* he had said, *this is not the way to love you.* Even though his raving words made no sense, she believed them. Later, she realized he wasn't right in the head, and the drugs made him worse. He smoked too much, took other drugs, and shot some into his veins. They left Daniel to his own.

"Are you staying for a while?" Annie asks.

"I don't think so," Tori says, taking another hit. This one tastes like day-old salad in her throat. A bad hit. She pulls her water bottle from her purse and tries to swallow the taste. "I have to get back."

"It's okay," Logan says. "Big college grad, we know you're not like us anymore."

Nothing could be closer and farther from the truth.

AT HOME TORI ARRANGES THE baggie of Nostalgia in a cedar box where she also keeps papers and a glass pipe with a rainbow flower blown onto it. She calls Kay and asks shur to come over. When shu arrives, shu has brought along a digital camera which shu hands to Tori like a holy relic. The camera is red and feels heavy in Tori's palm.

"It's neat," Tori says, thrusting it back at Kay. "Is it new?"

Kay won't take it back. Instead shu stands by Tori's side and shows her how to turn it on.

"It's for you," shu says. Shu arranges Tori's fingers over the buttons, uses Tori's hand like a puppet to take a photograph of the window in Tori's living room. "You have an eye for this," shu says. "Don't waste it."

"I can't take this," Tori says. It feels hard and slick and smells of new plastic. She hates the smell. She tries again to give it back, and when Kay won't take it, her fingers go limp. The camera falls to the carpet with a thud.

Kay leaves it where it has fallen. Takes Tori's hands in shur own and kisses the knuckles. "It's okay," shu says. "You don't have to." She lets shur lips graze the hairs on Tori's arms, kisses the mole on her neck, kisses her eyebrows, unbuttons her. Tori can tell shu wants to disrobe all of her, peel off her skin even, see inside her body like an X-ray. But Tori won't let shur.

Kay's body will change after shur operation. Tori isn't sure that she will be okay with this. Thinking of Kay's body as something she will have to get used to twice leaves her heavy in her stomach. Although she's familiar with the way a typical slate body looks post-op—she took a class on gender and sexuality at the university—she wishes she could have met shu once she was already complete, once shu had already grown into the new skin, the smooth Barbie V between shur legs. At least, Tori thinks, as she runs her hands over the flat chest, she has made a fascination, Kay got this part out of the way before we met.

"I won't know what to do with you," Tori whispers, "after the operation."

Kay's voice, usually calm, is hard-edged when shu responds. "What is that supposed to mean?"

Tori isn't one hundred percent sure. She laughs at herself. When is she ever?

"I just wish, you know, that we'd met once you were complete." She thinks it might help if she explains, but she can't seem to spit the words out. Not without time. She wishes she could freeze the moment and collect herself, but the world doesn't grant wishes that way.

"Complete?" Kay pushes Tori off shur chest. "I'm just as *complete* now as I'll ever be. I'll be more comfortable in my skin, sure, but I'm not incomplete. And besides," shu says, "you're one to talk. What are you doing with your life? You think your reason for living is so you can clean other people's messes?" Shu stops, though Tori can tell shu wants to go on. Then shu looks away. "I'm sorry," shu says. Shu doesn't wait for Tori to say anything, and Tori isn't sure she would say anything given the chance.

Once Kay has gone, Tori loads a bowl, tripping over the camera on her way back to bed. She kicks it underneath the couch. Her kick reminds her of the soccer ball she and her father used to pass back and forth out in the cool green grass until the chill on her bare feet became too much; her father would carry her inside and lower her onto the dry carpet. It's a memory empty of the sound of ice clinking in a glass, empty of the alcohol smell. She scrunches her toes against the carpet, a dirty shag she hasn't vacuumed in at least a month. It doesn't feel the same. If the world granted wishes, she would wish that it would feel the same.

THE BONFIRE IN TORI'S YARD is already blazing when Meredith skids into Tori's gravel drive on her Harley. It has been three days since Tori's fight with Kay, and she is surprised to see Meredith so soon after the last visit. It's surprising not to have to reacquaint herself; it's nice. The fire's warmth makes her bare legs burn.

"Long time no see," Tori says.

"I missed you," Meredith says.

Tori has known Meredith long enough to decipher this code. What she means to say is, she couldn't stand the thought of Tori with someone else. So, she has returned. Tori takes another hit in the hopes that she can convince herself that this time will be forever. They sit by the fire.

"Can't believe you still do this shit," Meredith says, lighting the bowl.

"And you don't?"

Meredith laughs. "I didn't say that. Just, you were always so smart, Tori. Smarter than any of us. I figured you'd grow up faster."

Tori doesn't want to think about it. She blows smoke from her nose. The burn makes her body tremble the way fingers will, later, when the two of them are once more wrapped in Tori's sheets. Tori recalls that first time, when Meredith pushed her onto her own bed. Took control of Tori's room without asking. Tori loved that she didn't ask. She felt in capable hands. They made love to B.B. King on repeat.

When they woke in the morning, the air was too hot for such closeness, but they clung to each other anyway. They turned off the music and let the noise of their breath soothe them back into fevered half-sleep.

"Where's the old gang?" Meredith dumps the cashed bowl into the fire. "Call them up."

Once Meredith left, there was nothing more to hold their group of college friends together, though during the five years of undergrad they spent every weekend together. Meredith had been glue, and none of them had ever noticed, not even Tori, who had felt her sticky sweat-soaked skin. But Tori still has their numbers.

An hour later, three chairs around the bonfire have filled with the warm bodies Tori used to cling to, sloppy with drink and smoke, as they stumbled home from evenings of smoke circles and study sessions, one-night stands and late-night movie marathons. When Daniel wouldn't stop calling, even two years after the breakup, it was these friends who, never having known him, demanded he leave her alone. Only two of their old gang is able to make it; the rest, like Meredith, moved away from Riddle after graduation. Still, looking from face to face around the fire is like looking four years into the past, and Tori's body hums, static building under skin. She wants nothing more than to run through the field surrounding her house, to float kites as Meredith scribbles poetry in her little black notebook. Always Tori used to wonder if Meredith was writing about her. Then, she knew she never was; instead, she wrote of the foreign places she disappeared to more and more those days. A fantastic life she hadn't asked Tori to be part of.

Once the beer has been drained and the empty bottles tossed into the fire in hopes that they will burst, once they have finished off the last of the Nostalgia, leaving only ash and a charred roach to burn, they sit back in their chairs and dream of running, though in reality none of them could summon the energy. The hum takes Tori over like an orgasm that never stops. She feels as if, for the first time since graduation, since she lost her place in this college town, she is home.

The hum intensifies. It vibrates her legs and creeps up into the space between her legs. For a moment she remembers Kay. Then forgets. Then it is Meredith again, Meredith's dimpled smile, her soft thighs. Music that she recognizes.

"Aren't you going to answer that?" Meredith slurs, clapping her hand over Tori's pants pocket, where Tori's phone has been ringing.

The phone feels strange in her sweaty palm, like an object that was never meant to be in this world. The caller ID tells her before she picks up that Logan's will be the voice on the other end of the line.

"I'm sorry," Logan says when she picks up. "I had to tell you. Daniel killed himself two weeks ago."

A wave of numb travels from her ear to her feet. Her stomach flops as if she has swallowed sour milk. She can feel Daniel all of a sudden. His hands like a bandage across her wrist, pulling her onto his bed while his parents were away. Refusing to let go of her hand in the night. Saying, *if something ever happened to you. If anyone ever hurt you.* And she knew, back then, that he was damaged. Had seen his own stepfather's dead body hanging from the ceiling. Had heard the fights from the other side of thin walls for all his childhood. She thought he was strong, thought he had grown from these experiences. *How*, she wanted and did not want to ask. So, she didn't. She could feel his lips down her neck and thought of how those lips would go blue-black in the earth.

"God," she says, as if she believes in Him. "How do you know?"

"His mom called me today. Got my number from his phone."

Meredith's hand grips her knee, travels up her leg. Tori doesn't think to stop her.

"Is there a funeral?"

"No. They had a secret funeral already. But we're having a memorial, next weekend. We're going to the barn. We'll say a few words about him, you know. We're meeting at my house. If you want to come. If you can stay a while."

"I'll be there," Tori says.

The phone goes quiet. Meredith doesn't ask who it was, what it was, and Tori moves her leg so that Meredith's hand falls away.

"What's up?" Meredith asks, crossing her arms across her chest.

"Daniel's dead. Killed himself."

Meredith's eyes widen. "Are you okay?" she asks.

"Will you go to the memorial with me next weekend?"

"I can't. I have a family thing next weekend, out of town. I already told them I'd go."

"Right." Tori nods, though what Meredith said seems strange, like déjà vu again. Tori remembers her grandfather's death, how her tears made Meredith anxious, how Meredith shrugged stiffly, told Tori she had to leave. That she had a family reunion to go to. Left Tori on the edge of her bed, clutching her own shaking body. "Right," Tori says.

Tori leaves the fire, goes inside, locks the door behind her. No one bothers her for hours, and when they do, she ignores the knocks, the pleas to please let them in to use the restroom. She googles Daniel's name. She finds an old arrest brief from Daniel's breaking-and-entering charge, which happened the year after college. Daniel had called her about it, drunk and sorry for himself. But there is no obituary, no news of a suicide. She searches for hours and finds nothing more, her fingers a fever on the keys, her mind a blank race of guilty thoughts. Could she have saved him? She wishes she had someone to tell her that she couldn't have. But it sounds as if, outside, the party has moved on.

It's the hour of nothing good when there is another knock at the door.

"Please open up," Kay says. "I'm sorry I snapped at you."

When Tori opens the door, Kay wraps shur arms around her. Tori shakes in her embrace. "What's wrong?" Kay asks, running shur hands through Tori's hair. "What happened?"

Tori tells her everything. "Doesn't it sound fishy?" she asks. "There's nothing, nothing at all online about him."

"It's weird, but maybe they just wanted to keep it secret. Don't tear yourself up about this, okay? Listen, I'll go with you, if you want, to the memorial."

Tori lets herself disappear beneath Kay's armpit. Breathes in the musk smell. She will let shur take care of her. Will let shur hold her and hide her from the light. Will let shur apologize for her and, yes, even love her.

HAVING GROWN UP IN THE city, Kay says during the drive down from Riddle, shu has never been in a town like Agape.

"As you can see, you're not missing much," Tori says as she navigates the car along the one road which curves like a snake through the small town, from the high school to the diner to the post office to the elementary to the gated community of houses which could fit five of Tori's tiny duplex within their walls. This is her past, laid bare without the itch in the throat, though Tori has brought along the last of her Nostalgia for the memorial.

"I bet you could take some great photographs here," Kay says as they pass the stone mega church. "Will the memorial be there?"

The memorial. For the length of the drive, she let herself forget, but now she must remember. Every bitter detail. There will be no turning around. For the last week she has felt on edge, always shaking in the night, looking every day for information, calling up old friends to see if they have heard. And no one else has.

"No," Tori says. "Not there."

To stop her shaking, and because she cannot, at the moment, go on to Logan's, Tori stops at the town's only coffee shop, a little place with crosses on the walls and in a jewelry case at the front counter. The young man behind the counter is someone Tori used to know, an old friend. Jaden. She wonders why, smart boy like him, he never got out of this place.

"How are you?" he asks, smiling briefly at Kay before looking back to Tori. Kay stands with shur arms in shur jacket pockets.

Tori shrugs. "Okay enough, considering the occasion."

"What occasion?"

He doesn't know, she realizes with cold dread. Although he and Daniel were never best friends, were never lovers, they were close. As if shu can read her, Kay grabs her hand.

"Daniel's dead," Tori says. "Killed himself."

"What? When was this?" Jaden says.

"Three weeks ago."

He laughs. The sound is a fire alarm. When he realizes Tori isn't laughing with him, he opens his mouth, shuts it. "I saw Daniel at the general store last night. He was fine."

Cold dread is becoming as familiar as a fever. Because this news is neither good nor bad; it moves into her gut and twists her insides.

"Excuse me," she says, and she rushes from the coffee shop, the door's jingle a throb in her head. Beside the car, she calls Logan. He answers on the first ring.

"Where are you?" he asks. "You're late. The rest of the gang is here already. We're ready to go."

"Daniel's alive," Tori says. "Jaden says they saw him last night, at work."

"That's impossible," Logan says.

"I'm telling you, I just saw Jaden, and he says Daniel is one-hundred-percent fine."

"We're all here. Waiting for you. Just come on. It'll be like old times. We can't know for certain. Let's just have the memorial, go out to the barn, share some bowls. Say a few words. In honor of Daniel. I mean, his mom called me. She called me the day it happened, a week ago. She was crying. There's no way she was faking that."

"A week ago," Tori says. And she knows then not to argue. She hangs up. Kay has joined her beside the car, and without explaining where they're going, they climb in. Tori drives. She remembers the way; she would remember it with her eyes closed. Back then she took this road out of mind. She is out of mind again, and no drug has passed through her system since the night before, when Kay watched her smoke a bowl of Nostalgia to black.

Daniel's father's house is stone, situated back from the road and surrounded by lean live oaks. The yard is dark, and as they walk hand in hand up the gravel path Tori's heart hyperventilates in her chest. Before they reach the door, a man emerges, his arms crossed.

"Can I help you?"

"We're looking for Daniel," Tori says. She doesn't know if Daniel's father will remember her. If he knows that she was the first woman to strip him down and take him into her mouth, to crawl on top of him and initiate him into the world of lovers. That she has regretted that decision, and not only because Daniel wasn't ready, not only because Daniel blamed her for losing himself. "I'm an old friend. I had dinner here once." Matzo balls in broth. Toast and steamed Brussels sprouts.

"Not really, but my memory's not all it used to be. Daniel's in his room, up there. Do you want me to go get him?"

Tori's body wilts. Relief. She thinks about the last time she saw him, his hair tangled, clothes baggy and torn, eyes bloodshot. The memories overwhelmed her like a drug, and it was because of him that she no longer frequented Agape unless she needed had to. Unless she needed Nostalgia shoved into clear plastic baggies.

"No, thanks," she says. "I'm tired of rehashing. But he's not dead?"

"Dead? No, Daniel's not dead. Why?"

"A friend lied to me," she says.

"Doesn't sound like a friend to me." Daniel's father's arms have come uncrossed, and Tori isn't sure when in the conversation it happened, but it seems to signal some small degree of remembrance. And what else could she ask for but to be remembered?

"Yeah," she says. "Thanks so much. Don't tell Daniel I was here, please."

The man nods. "I remember you," he says. "I won't."

Tori and Kay turn and walk from the driveway, slower this time, Tori listening to the crunch of their footsteps on the path. Kay's hand in hers makes her feel safe, as if Kay could protect her, if she needed it, which she doesn't.

They don't go to Logan's. Tori deletes his number from her phone, as she did Daniel's long ago. Later she will block it, too. She is not mad at him. She understands the urge to hold on, to keep the people who were once close nearby. To relive that which you remember in a hazy euphoria. Instead, she and Kay drive home, where they sit beside the fire and look, without speaking, into the waves of heat lifting to the sky like a mirage in the air. Tori doesn't load a bowl.

Kay snaps a picture of her in the firelight; when developed, it will show her body dark as night. She will not be smiling, though there will be a rosy fire glow on her cheeks.

"Can I?" Tori asks.

"So long as you don't drop it." Kay grins. Shur grin splits shur face like a crack to let light in.

The camera feels like her pipe in Tori's palm, the same weight.

IT WILL NOT BE EASY, Tori thinks, to stop. She will want to remember. Her photographs, then. She will capture the places she once loved, the people she will try to love in new ways. She opens the box on her desk and spreads the remaining Nostalgia across a blank piece of paper. Arranges it to form a picture; a figure with no shape, no curves, no breasts, no genitals. Not too bad, she thinks. I can get used to it, she thinks.

The flash lightning cuts the room in half. Dots swim before Tori's eyes. She hopes the picture will come out, but there's no way to know until she develops it in the art building's darkroom. It's a beautiful feeling, to see and not see what the future will bring.

WHEN EMMA MOVED TO OREGON with her girlfriend, she left part of herself behind. Her parents inhabited a two-story on eight acres in Riddle, Texas, where Emma had lived for the whole of her life. Oregon was an adventure. After all, she couldn't rely on family forever. Here was a chance at a new family, built from the ground up. Emma seized it. But when she and Lin arrived at the rent house in Oregon, Emma realized she was missing half her body.

The hard part was getting out of the U-haul with one arm and one leg. Lin hoisted Emma down and let Emma lean on her as they hobbled through the front door. She leaned Emma against the wall and carried in a chair from the truck.

"Thanks," Emma said. "Guess I found a way out of unpacking."

Neither was sure how they'd gone so long without realizing that Emma was missing a half. They'd been in the

U-haul for three days straight, stopping along the way at roadside rest stops and gas stations, but Emma, who with each mile had grown more lethargic, didn't once leave the truck. She ate and drank little and had not felt the need to urinate. Since Lin stocked up on Red Bull and caffeine pills, she never wanted for more sleep than she could squeeze out in a power nap and didn't think of relinquishing the reins to Emma. They'd had every excuse not to realize Emma's condition.

At the house, however, they were caught by the delicacy of the situation. With half a body, Emma lacked the strength she'd possessed before. She wasn't able to lift her suitcase, let alone help lug the couch indoors. The neighbor boys offered to help, for a fee.

"What happened to *her?*" they asked when they saw Emma, half her head in her one hand.

"I'm sick," she said with half her lips.

With the furniture inside, the house looked more like home. From her chair, Emma surveyed their belongings: a couch, four of Lin's metal sculptures, their dining table and four wood chairs, boxes upon boxes of dishes and appliances, all marked with Sharpie: FRAGILE. Lin's belongings looked strange mixed with her own.

Lin took the truck back and returned with a cane from a local gas station: black wood, ornamented at the top with a grinning lion's head.

"I thought it would help you adjust," Lin said as she helped Emma hobble from room to room, showing her the places they would hang Emma's artwork and the corners in which they might place Lin's sculptures. Over the years Emma had spent most of her money on friends' art, bright red and blue abstracts, a portrait of a fairy poised to disappear into the labial wound of a tree trunk. Now she would hang them on new walls.

Lin led Emma to the bedroom, where the mattress lay on the floor surrounded by boxes. They sat on its edge. Lin pressed her hand to Emma's cheek and looked into her one blue eye. "You'll learn to love it as much as I love you," Lin said.

Lin kissed her, half her lips pressed against Emma's, half against air.

THE HALF OF EMMA LEFT at her parents' was the half that bled. As the truck journeyed north, Emma's other half appeared piece by piece in the driveway, until one morning Emma's mom found Emma's other half curled in a ball on the concrete. Emma's other half forced herself to stand, unfolding her body as if it were a wrinkled sweater. She felt as though she'd been ripped at the seams. She pressed her fingers into her side and felt stringy tissue and loose skin. Her hand was bloody when she pulled it away. In ten minutes, a thin film of flesh spread over the wounds.

Her mom cupped her hand around Emma's other half's shoulder. "Don't worry," she said. "You'll be back one of these days."

Emma's other half shrugged. "I don't care."

No one, not even Emma's clueless older sister, brain fogged by the baby in her belly, was fooled.

Emma shivered in her childhood bed, and the things that used to bring her comfort—taking a bath, eating a whole batch of chocolate cookies in one go, even her friend Mike's art show—no longer made her happy. Her melancholy wasn't due to the absence of half her body, not literally; it was the hole in her bones, as though she would never be the same again. It was also the absence of Lin. She'd grown used to Lin's smell, oily and old as Lin's thrift store jacket. Without that smell in her blanket, she could not sleep.

Her family tried to cheer her up. She wished for their sake it would work. Her mom bought old movies for her to watch, comedies, *humor helps the healing process*, and her dad tried to interest her in jigsaw puzzles and thick black beer after dinner. Her sister invited her to shop for baby clothes, and though seeing her sister fondle the pastel fabrics made Emma's other half hopeful for the future, it didn't take her mind away from the thought of Lin's hands buried in Emma's hair.

One night Emma's father took her aside after dinner.

"If you need to go, go. We'll understand," he said.

Emma's other half shook her head. "I want to stay."

For she knew that for all her missing Lin, leaving wouldn't help. Sure, having Lin around made her family, their bickering and pestering, bearable, but the opposite was also true. Without her family, Emma would have no reprieve from the intensity of her love for Lin. Because while her love for her family was the kind of love which heals and understands, her love for Lin was so hectic she sometimes feared it would scald what was left of her skin.

THREE THOUSAND MILES AWAY, EMMA coped better with the loss. She wasn't immune to feeling like less of a person, but she faked it. She didn't, after all, want Lin to feel as though she had ruined her life when it had been Emma's decision to come. Lin had done an excellent job with the house. Their things, so many things, filled each cranny of each room, overflowed from the cabinets and the closets. Tapestries served as curtains, pinned to the wall with pushpins, and all they wanted for were cleaning supplies.

Lin had a shop out back for sculpting paraphernalia, her posters of the classics pinned to the walls: Cupid and Psyche, The Kiss. Her slabs of metal rods, soldering iron for piecing together her metal birds and bees, her welder for the bigger pieces. She'd moved to teach at the university, a worthy job for a sculptor as inexperienced with the world of academia as she. When Emma imagined Lin before a classroom of eager students, she was proud to be hers.

At home, Emma gardened. She'd grown used to getting around with the help of the cane and discovered that she loved nothing more than digging in the wet dirt as the constant drizzle wet her hair. At first, the rain bugged her, but she soon realized that without the rain the garden would not be as green, and neither would the evergreens which lined every street be as thick and tall. This was the trees' territory; Emma was happy to share it.

Eventually, there were no more rose bushes to prune, no more blackberries in the alley to thin, no more winter flowers to plant, and Emma ran out of tasks to do. She stood in Lin's workshop, watching her attach the stem of a recycled metal dandelion with her welding torch. A break in the flame allowed her to clear her throat. Lin turned and lifted the shield of her mask. "You make me nervous standing there. Why don't you look for a job?" she said. "Something to get out of the house, settle in place."

"Who would hire me?"

"There's something out there for everyone."

Emma searched the personals until she found a job at a chocolate raisin factory. Emma's job was to pull three levers four times a day, once in the morning, once at lunch, once after lunch, and once in the evening. If there was ever an emergency, the manager told her, she would be the most integral part of the team.

The first two levers were black and powered the line and the mechanical dealimabobs that poured the chocolate. The third lever was yellow, the paint chipped. No one knew what it powered.

"No one's known since the factory changed hands, back in the 70s," the manager told Emma with a shrug. "Just pull it."

While waiting to pull the levers, Emma tried to link up with her other half. She closed her eye tight until she felt her lid strain. She concentrated until her head pounded and opened her mouth and breathed out all the words she wanted to tell herself.

She never got a reply.

●●

EMMA'S FAMILY RECEIVED THE MESSAGES from Emma's mind; they flooded in through the phone, a string of words with no breath. When they tried to respond to the ramble, their response went ignored, the phone clicked, the connection ended. They wrote the messages on a pad. Emma's other half ignored them. Emma's mother and sister called Emma to check up on occasion but never talked for long; they were busy, and talking to Emma made them sad. Emma and her father talked every week, always in private. Her father knew Emma's other half would feel threatened. Even the name spoken sent her into a sulk, no matter which half it was spoken about. They talked about the factory and the weather, safe subjects that would not remind them they were far apart. He told Emma that her other half was unhappy. Emma tried to seem ambivalent. If her other half wouldn't respond to the messages Emma's father swore he passed on, Emma couldn't be expected to care.

Emma's father was an inventor who had achieved success from a cat collar that squirted water when the cat jumped on the counters. Unbeknownst to Emma, his most successful invention was a lever that would transmit the emotional energy of the environment in which it was placed back to company headquarters. The raisin factory's headquarters had long ago closed, so its data fed back into her father's lab. He could tell from the smell of the data that Emma was on the other side.

He had recently finished another invention: an artificial system of limbs that would allow Emma's other half to walk without assistance. The metal wrapped around her neck and hips, and the metal arm and leg, which stored the energy exerted from her real limbs, were thick and sturdy enough to allow her to run and swim, which was good because the summer was hotter than it had ever been before. She finally gained the nerve to see her friends again. They touched the cool metal of her father's new invention and envied her robot parts.

"You're like the Terminator," Mike had said.

Her family noticed a change right away. When her mother suggested Emma work with one of the family's friends, she agreed. The woman was a local jewelry maker, and Emma's other half's new arm allowed her to string beads at an alarming rate, and to knot the knots tighter than any human hand.

After a while she created her own designs. She paid no rent to her parents, and every penny earned went back to her beads. She strung bracelets with beads that jangled and beads that clanked against one another and made songs of glass. Eventually she made enough to sell some, but she had no one to sell them to save the jewelry maker, who bought them at ten percent above cost and displayed them as part of her own collection. Emma had all the business savvy; she was the one who would have been able to entice others into buying the bracelets.

"Do you miss her?" Emma's mom asked one night after dinner over her famous ice cream brownie sundaes. Beside Emma's other half, a bracelet lay half-finished: E-M-M, read the letter beads.

Emma's other half didn't answer.

"I do," said her sister. "I wish I knew she'd come home eventually, but what if she doesn't?"

"She will." Emma's dad scooped fudge into his mouth. It dribbled down his chin. He didn't wipe it away. "Don't you worry."

That night Emma's other half drank down two icy glasses of whiskey. She filled the glass again. The ice melted and turned the drink lentil brown. She sat on the first step of her parents' porch and looked up at the stars, clear as glass. Most of her parents' live oaks were dead of rot. Their bare branches reached out for Emma's other half's hand. If they hadn't been so far away, she would have taken their handshake or let them lift her onto them with their scratchy grip and bring her as close to the stars as she would ever be. She had always been afraid of climbing trees.

IN OREGON, EMMA HAD TREES to climb aplenty and soon found a new love of climbing the apple tree in her backyard to eat the apples, letting the naked cores fall to the ground. She would eat until she'd ruined her dinner. Lin scolded her, in jest, but really Lin loved that she had found niches for herself in the glum of rain.

At the school, Lin made friends with whom she shared drinks after work. Her sculptures grew more intricate and skilled. But at night when she came home and

Emma was weeding or pruning the apple tree from the inside out with her long-handed scissors, Lin cried. The first time Emma heard Lin's hiccup sobs, she was fascinated by the ache in her own stomach. It was one of these nights beside Lin that Emma realized she hadn't cried since she left her other half behind. In fact, she hadn't felt one surge of sadness. She had looked on the trees and felt joy, she surely had felt a brutal ambivalence, but pain had disappeared.

Confused, fascinated by this, too, as she was fascinated by so much these days, Emma tried to hurt herself. She fell from the tree. Her body cracked when she landed, but when she woke from the blackout on the couch, nothing was broken, nothing twisted, and Lin had been the whole time by her side. She told Lin she didn't love her; when Lin's quivering expression became too much, Emma pulled her close and admitted it was a lie.

"Sometimes I wish I didn't," Emma said. "I could go home to my family."

She found it odd she could see and experience the pain in her girlfriend's eyes but not her own body. Suddenly her skin felt foreign to her, and the numbness spread from her brain to her foot. At work she didn't pull the yellow lever. Nothing happened. No one noticed.

PAIN WASN'T HARD TO COME by for Emma's other half. While the metal half made life easier, it also made her real half sore. Every step sent a shock up her spine, a needle into her muscles. Her father told her she would get used to it. She did not tell him about the bruises that had appeared, after Emma's fall from the tree, down her body like purple birthmarks. She cursed Emma for leaving, and for not realizing that her pain affected them both; at times she thought she hated that half of her guts. Other times she wished she could trade places.

When she felt the resentment boil, she went to bars. She met women, and men, who seemed interesting, interested. They would run their hands down her metal arms, cool to the touch; they found her unsettling and exotic. She always mentioned Lin. They weren't turned away. Once Emma's other half said Lin's name, however, she wanted nothing more than to go home alone.

She spent most of her time with her family. Her sister had her baby. The labor was quick, and once the cord was cut, the blood cleaned away, Emma's other half held her nephew. As she looked down at the boy, she couldn't believe her luck.

Here she was, able to share this moment with her sister. The baby a full person, both his halves intact.

In the weeks that followed, her father worked all day on a two-part device that could transmit vocal waves to cats from the human mouth, and vice versa: the Mewmaker, he called it. He hoped to perfect and alter the device to work on children, to help his other daughter abandon more quickly her sleepless baby nights. But he couldn't get the device to translate his words correctly; the cat always did the opposite of what he told it.

Just like his daughter.

He tried to tell Emma's other half to find the joy, but pain seemed to be all she focused on. The disappointment of Emma not being there for her nephew's birth soon overtook the delight of him. The pain of walking masked the joy of it. The only solace was her bracelets, the one for Emma still unfinished, and her family, who, without Emma, even in the presence of a new life, seemed half as lively, half as loved.

LIN HAD ALSO BEEN TO bars in secret. This was one of the reasons she cried. She'd met a woman there one night, though they'd only gone as far as the parking lot before Lin lost it and left without her. It was far enough. She'd known something was missing since the day Emma left the truck less of a woman; in the parking lot, Lin realized that she needed that missing piece. Because Emma wasn't Emma without her fear of trees. Emma wasn't Emma without her fits of sadness, and Emma wasn't Emma without her kooky father, her silent mother, her over-determined sister. She wasn't Emma without the love for cheap liquor. She wasn't Emma without her other half.

There were the physical implications of her condition to consider as well. She had one breast, the one without the single freckle at the nipple. She had half a posterior, and though her body had improvised in terms of the less savory aspects of bodily functions, half a posterior didn't elicit the same sexual response in Lin. And she only had half a vagina, which gave her less pleasurable skin, only half a clitoris, and less room for error.

Emma didn't know why Lin cried. She could feel the absence of her other half like a ghost limb, but she never thought that Lin could miss the qualities in herself she had always wished she could leave behind.

Without her knowledge, Lin called Emma's other half.

"I've missed you," she said.

At first Emma's other half didn't speak.

"Say my name," Lin said.

"Lin," Emma's other half said. "It's been fucking hard without you."

They talked every day. Lin called her on breaks and on her way home from work. They whispered like lovers, scared of being overheard.

EMMA'S OTHER HALF CAUGHT HER father during one of his own calls to Emma.

"Who are you talking to?" she asked.

"You." Her father smiled. Then, seeing the anger on his daughter's face, he hung up. "What's the matter?"

"How could you?"

Calling Emma was more difficult after that; always Emma's other half's eye remained watchful. Though she carefully monitored her family's phone usage, she continued to carry out her own telephone affair with Lin. "I don't know how I'm supposed to do this," she often said. How Lin had missed the melodrama. No, not missed, but noticed the absence of with a wash of nausea; things would never be the same, and Lin's life with Emma was inexplicably altered, forever, without her permission.

Her Emma at home didn't find out on her own. She never snooped, never tried to pry under Lin's skin. Not like her other half, who demanded the messy details of Lin's every move. Emma didn't notice that Lin had stopped crying, that her phone bill had risen. Instead Lin told Emma what was happening, an attempt to rattle her. "I've been talking to your other half."

"Oh?" Emma was chopping a carrot but didn't falter. "How is she?"

"She misses me. Us. Your sister had her baby."

Emma stopped. "I leave messages. She doesn't answer."

"You do? She doesn't?"

Emma shook her head. "My sister had her baby?" She frowned. "Why didn't they call me?"

Lin shrugged, unsure of what to say. Emma continued chopping. Lin left the room without a word. Half an hour later she returned with two sheets of paper. "We're going home for Thanksgiving."

WITHOUT HER FAMILY TELLING HER, Emma's other half knew they were on their way. She felt the tug of her skin tighten as the plane crept closer, and though Emma in the air did not feel a popping in her ears, Emma's other half had to chew a whole pack of gum to rid herself of the pressure. For an hour during their layover in Denver, Emma's other half itched so badly she had to take a hot bath in the hopes that it would stop. It didn't stop. Not even when they'd arrived.

The house looked different to Emma. The smell was foreign but familiar, her parents' carpet mixed with the cat hair, the pungent garlic from her mother's cooking, the lemon and vinegar of the kitchen counter. The rooms looked larger than she remembered, the brown of the walls lighter, her sister fatter, her parents older. She'd missed so much.

Her sister hugged her close as she could. "Your nephew," she said, pushing the child into Emma's arm. Emma looked down into the baby's face and felt as though she knew him already, a déjà vu. But in the pit of her stomach lay an emptiness she easily found the name for: regret. Because she hadn't, in fact, met him before, hadn't been there for his birth, and would never have the opportunity to remedy that mistake.

Emma's other half ignored Emma at first, jealous of the attention. Her skin still itched, but she'd grown used to it. After dinner, which she took in her bedroom, and after most everyone had gone to bed, Emma's other half emerged. She found Emma and Lin on the couch with their father, and she stood for a while silent in the doorway. They were talking about Oregon, about the twin rivers that ran through their city, about the pristine coast with water so cold you turned blue if you touched it. There was a spot by the river, Emma said, where she went sometimes to think after work. The width of the river made her forget she was only halfway complete.

They all knew Emma's other half was there before she spoke. "I've dreamt of that."

Emma looked at Emma. Emma's other half approached and slid into the folds of the couch. With her other half, it was easier for her to talk openly. Before long the room emptied around Emma and Emma.

"How do you do it?" Emma asked. "Live away from the ones you love?"

"How do you?"

"Carefully," they said.

IN THE NIGHT THEY SLEPT with Lin between them. They felt like she was inside of them, as much part of their body as each other. In the morning, they were woken by the smell of turkey, buttery and rich, of peach cobbler baking in the oven. At dinner, Emma and Emma shared one plate but piled it twice as high. Emma's other half showed Emma her bracelets. She promised to finish the one for her.

Emma knew then that they could never again be one. The wounds in Emma's other half's sides had sealed. Already, they had grown without the other, had learned to walk without the help of others. Already, they had found new loves they would not bear to part with: beads and trees and rain. With Thanksgiving Emma had been lucky to have the money and the time to come home. As in the case of her nephew's birth, she wouldn't always be so lucky; not every big event would wait for her. Things would change, people would die without warning, and Emma wouldn't be there for all of it.

But part of her would. Part of her needed to be, or else she would never forgive herself all the missed memories she would suffer.

BEFORE EMMA AND LIN LEFT, Emma's father led her into his chaotic laboratory, experiments abandoned and escaped, shattered glass glinting on the counters, cat posters on all the walls, and in the corner of the room, under a box of glass, a yellow lever. He told Emma to place her hand on it. The metal was cold and smelled like copper. She could feel the emptiness of the room distant on the other side; the factory was on holiday.

"I've made some changes, made it so it goes both ways. Every day you can pull it, and every day Emma will wait here until you do. You'll be able to communicate this way, like you were side by side."

EMMA'S OTHER HALF STAYED BEHIND when they drove her to the airport. She wasn't good with goodbyes.

On the plane Emma couldn't wait to get back. She missed her garden; she knew weeds would have choked some of the flowers, and the roses would be stunted with neglect. She thought about her place by the river, how the rocks had been made smooth by the current, how the landscape was always changing. How it would keep changing. How one day she might not recognize it. Until that day, she could only be happy to be home.

WE ALL MAKE MISTAKES. As I sit on the floor of my bedroom, surrounded by the journals I kept in high school and in my twenties and fill out the doctor's form, I tally mistakes in the corner of the paper. Before marriage, before Dover and I's quiet nights trading words and sharing thoughts between binged television episodes, relationships were tumultuous. My tallies reflect this. Particularly the final tally, the one that got me into this mess to begin with. The doctor didn't ask me for a tally, just brief descriptions of all sexual encounters, mistakes or not, to jog my memory along with the age at which I experienced them. But I need to prove to myself that the dissolution of my marriage wasn't unique, that it hadn't been a surprise. I should have seen it coming.

●●

NOTES ON SEVERAL PIECES OF PARTLY-CRUMPLED PAPER, CRINKLED WITH COFFEE STAINS

#1 (AGE 16)

Anne, the first woman I made love to, tasted like sunlight and sweat. We kissed behind a half-open door at the house where she lived with her father and stepmother. Afterward we went for Chinese food. We were together, off-and-on, for two years. We lied and cheated and searched through one another's texts. We cooked each other Foreman grill chicken and pasta with four types of cheese. We raised one another in homes where we otherwise went unnoticed.

#2 (AGE 18)

I lost my virginity twice. First, with the woman of sunlight and sweat and a Superman tattoo across her back. Second, with Mario, a Czech cigarette smoker, a college boy, a smooth talker who asked me to be his girlfriend after knowing me for one day.

We fucked in hotel rooms. We ate Whataburger after. We smoked weed from a pipe that looked like a metal cigarette and performed rainy picnics in the park. The sex was a beautiful pain. He told me I would leave him for a woman. I left him for Anne; she no longer tasted like sunlight and sweat when she begged me to come back.

"I slept with my ex, too," he said when I told him. "I don't even care."

#3 (AGE 18)

I wasn't done with men's beautiful pain. The third person I slept with, Daniel, was a latent schizophrenic with hippy hair and a wallet stuffed with acid hits. Lucifer in the sky with diamonds, dancing half-naked in the front yard of a friend's house while his parents were on vacation.

He said he wanted to take it slow. I waited a week to ask for what I wanted; for me a week was slow. Not for him. After we broke up, we argued about timing during his late-night surprise appearances at my door. He told me I'd get pregnant before the year was out. He called for five years after I stopped answering. On my 23rd birthday, I changed my number.

#4 (AGE 18)

It wasn't good. I squeezed my eyes shut. It wasn't good.

#5 (AGE 18)

We both had boyfriends when we first met in that final raging year of high school. Natalie gave me a massage on a crowded downtown street. Once we were both in college, she called again. I went to her without a thought. We sat in her apartment, as far across the couch from one another as possible, but when I got up to leave, she shoved me against the door and kissed me harder than I'd ever been kissed.

I kneaded her soft thighs in her cozy bed. She rescued me from a bad drunk in the company of my *Dungeons & Dragons* friends. I puked in her stripper shoes. We drank mimosas in my dorm. She only called me when she got lonely.

#6 (AGE 18)

I remember Christopher crisp as a Facebook photo: red curls, a single mole on his neck, an affinity for exclamation. I met him at a NORML meeting, which I attended in the hopes of finding a new dealer. The redhead didn't deal but kept a six-foot bong on his mantle.

He quoted scenes from *Catch-22*, pillow talk with a prostitute. I watched him play football games on his Wii. We played beer pong with his friends. Once I puked in his sink: spaghetti with mushrooms and peppermint ice cream. Every time he asked me over, I went. Then he stopped asking.

#7 (AGE 19)

So, I fucked his friend Simon over a game of strip poker.

"Pretty good for a dude, huh?" he said. It wasn't.

#8 (AGE 19)

Simon's friend Oliver was better, a sweet blond who wrote bad poetry and lived in a private dorm next to Anne's college apartment. I visited him after Anne. I visited Anne after him, soaking wet from rain. The cookie taste of him still lingered on my lips when I slipped my tongue between her legs.

"What do you want?" the blond asked.

I didn't lie. "I want Anne to leave her girlfriend and come back to me."

"Then we have no business being together."

#9 (AGE 19)

But Anne didn't love me anymore. I sweated out her sunlight in the dark of my room in the house I shared with two roommates, a dozen fevers moving through me with no further explanations. When I was well again, I befriended Anne and her girlfriend, Cathryn, and Anne's roommate, Dana, who was fucking Cathryn, too.

I didn't tell Anne that I drove each weekend to swallow bitter pills and fuck a blue-haired candy kid, Xander, king of the club. His last name remains unknown. We had nightly phone sex. I drove an hour to be in his bed every now and again and stayed as long as it took to finish. He knew nothing about me. It was easier to delete his number when Anne came calling, came crying. She had found out about Cathryn and Dana.

We moved Anne out of her apartment and into the home I shared. She wrote "I love you" in paint on my desk. We didn't make it official.

#10 (Age 19)

At least that was my excuse when I met the most beautiful woman I've ever loved, cherry cheeks and gruff throat and the cutest drunk smile I've ever seen. Meredith and I kissed for the first time in a dance club against the red brick of a pillar.

It was time to leave the sunshine behind, but we always hold on to first love longer than we should.

Too drunk, we wound up on a bare mattress in an empty room in the house I now shared with Anne. We woke to Anne screaming in the door. I didn't remember a thing.

After a long night of fighting, I pledged myself to Anne. I tried to be friends with those cherry cheeks, tried to keep her around, but Meredith left my house one night and said she wouldn't come back.

I cut ties with Anne the next day in a brief tearless goodbye. I loved Meredith even when she told me she was moving up north. We didn't last that long. Even before she moved, her clothes smelled like Anne's ex-girlfriend Cathryn, my first enemy, my only enemy. When Meredith begged me back, I stood my ground.

#11 (Age 19)

Nothing counts on Halloween. Especially not a woman you forget before you even know her.

#12 (Age 19) & #13 (Age 19)

Once upon a time I loved a woman who smelled like sunshine. Later she loved a woman with long hair and a dark past who would become an enemy and a friend;

isn't there a word for that? They lived with Dana, the daughter of a pastor. Dana and Cathryn, they were made for each other, or at least for that part of their lives.

I had taken a lover when I had a lover, first with Daniel, then with Meredith. Did I deserve full-circle? Cathryn was so full of mystery no one could resist her, Meredith least of all. I didn't want Cathryn. I was the only one. But Dana was a beauty in her dark apartment where I rode my bike as soon as she heard about our girlfriends' liaisons in party bathrooms.

"It's okay," I said to Dana.

"Fucking bitch," she said.

We ate burgers and went our separate ways. One night later Dana and Cathryn were back together. Meredith and I stayed apart. I fucked Dana and Cathryn both instead, in a room with no curtains on the windows. Pushed and pulled between the woman I wanted and the woman I hated, I didn't belong. *I'm lost*

#14 (AGE 19)

"Women," I said, collapsing onto a grungy old couch at a college party. Hunter overheard me and commiserated. I gave him my number when he asked. He read poetry like he was being held at gunpoint, a disorienting rise in his voice leading to a climax that never came. He lived in a trailer full of trash and secrets. He ate food he didn't like to impress me. I saw him in public once and left quickly.

Meredith moved to Colorado, and I cried a lot.

That was the end of the poet and me.

#15 (AGE 19)

Jeremiah was covered in tattoos. When he asked me to dinner, I never went, but I showed up at his apartment late at night to smoke weed and get naked. He left the TV on all the time, and I heard Charlie Sheen's crazy laugh as I fucked him. Too much noise is still too much noise, and when I left, I never came back.

#16 (AGE 20)

Here is where I tried again. Here is where I walked with a man eight years my senior who didn't know what he wanted and wanted what he didn't know. Michael and I played board games on his carpet. I wanted him all the time and he couldn't give that much of himself. I was in a hurry, wanted to move too fast, wanted to get the hard parts out of the way, wanted to experience it all then and there and he drank too much anyway.

#17 (Age 20)

But I did miss him, and Michel's name was one letter away. He had brown curls and deep Italian brown eyes and his eyes looked sunken into his face when he was tired and every time I saw him, he was tired. The first time was beautiful when I woke up in bed beside him, sunlight creeping in through a little crack in the window.

The second time, he moved his head in circles. When we finished, he jumped on his computer and played video games as though I wasn't there.

#18 (Age 20) *oh he dead*

It was Grayson I wanted, a boy who left hickeys all over my neck. A friend of a best friend. A bowl cut, like the Beatles.

When I got too drunk, I asked Grayson to walk me back. I stumbled under a tree and he caught me, kissed me. We snuck into my house.

"Your bed's full of books," he said. I pushed them off. I'd been sleeping alone for weeks.

"You and your girls," he said.

"Boys, too," I said. I kissed him again.

I don't remember the rest. I blacked out. He left before sunrise. The next day I heard nothing from him. At a friend's place a week later, he called his new girlfriend by my name.

His friend Eliot looked nothing like him. He kissed me on the couch in the room where Grayson sat with his new girlfriend. He drove me to his place without asking if that was where I wanted to go.

#19 (Age 20)

I waited because they told me I should wait. The violinist was hard to get. Her name was Dover.

"Like the cliffs?" I said, when she introduced herself in the middle of my roommate's party.

"Got any weed?" she said.

She was sitting in my house like she belonged there, crosslegged in my dining table chair with her ponytail and her bright red leather pants.

"No," I said. "What kind of guest doesn't bring their own weed?"

But when she asked my roommate for my number, I relented.

The first time we made love, we were in a lake at a state park, past the time we were supposed to be in the water. She commented each night on the moon and its changes. She offered up everything I never wanted to lose.

I loved her with everything I had to lose.

When I lost her, ten years after we took our vows, I lost everything I loved.

#20 (AGE 35)

There are a million excuses I could give. Fifteen years of monogamy pass, and you start to itch for the excitement of a stranger's hands, for the unraveling of a mystery, peeling back their words to reveal what's really underneath. You feel unwanted, after years of being looked at with the gentler gaze of long-term lust. You feel the need to return to that younger self.

You're a worthless piece of shit. You're everything you never wanted to be.

IN THE OFFICE OF THE DOCTOR WITH NO DEGREES ON THE WALLS

"That's everyone?" the doctor asks.

"Yes," I say. "It's a lot, isn't it?"

"Do you feel like it's a lot?"

"Oh, come on. It's a lot."

"Huh." The doctor taps her pen against her clipboard.

"Then it must be a lot."

"Honestly? You think so?"

"Honestly, Ms. Underwood?"

I nod.

"I've seen more."

I shift in my seat, cross and uncross my legs, wipe my sweating palms on my thighs.

"That's everyone, you said? Are you very sure?"

"Yes. I kept good records."

"That's everyone you experienced penetration with in any of its forms? That's a finger in the vagina, the anus. A finger in the mouth. A penis in the mouth. A tongue in the vagina. You want as many as possible."

Fuck. Blowjobs. Blowjobs probably counted. I hadn't recorded all of those encounters in my journals, not as meticulously.

"That's all of them," I say.

She studies my notes. "The good news is you didn't leave a lot of time between them. That's good. Fewer gaps means smaller steps." She scribbles something on her form.

"You remember how this works?"

"Yes."

"Tell me. Say it back to me. I want to be sure."

"The memories are a map, right? I follow memory to memory. Each one is like a stepping stone."

"Yes, that's fairly accurate. Are you certain you got everyone? As I said, you want as many stones as possible so that you do not fall through."

"What happens if I fail?"

"You must start again."

"That's all? I won't die or get lost or go into a coma or something?"

"You start over. This means we start from the beginning. Your fee covers one attempt. If you can pay again, we can go again. But I suspect you cannot pay again."

I think of my bank account, that red number. I pulled it all to come here. I sold off the violinist's violin.

"You assume correctly," I say.

She hands me the clipboard.

"Is there anyone you want to add?"

I add three oral-only encounters. She takes the clipboard back. It's not everyone, but it's as close as I can get.

"Much better," she says.

THE MACHINE LOOKS LIKE AN MRI, but it closes over my head like a coffin. It whirs around me, strange lights flashing in my eyes until I squeeze them shut.

"Don't," the doctor says over the speaker. "You need to follow the light with your eyes."

I follow it back-and-forth, back-and-forth.

"It's not working," I say.

"Wait for it."

I wait. "I don't feel anything," I say.

"Wait—"

And then, yes, there it is: that smell of sunlight in my nostrils. The graze of my nose on skin so pale it's as though it's never seen the sun. We're in Anne's sloppy bed at her parents' house, behind a closed door that her stepmother will later scold us for closing.

She is thrashing underneath me, but I know from the future that she's faking it.

I faked it, too, sometimes. I grip her skin and remember why I loved her. But, also, why I stopped. Even this first time, there is a lie beneath the surface. So many lies. So much work to pry them apart. An onion that's rotting underneath.

Afterward we lay in one another's arms and giggle and kiss all the empty spaces. "It won't always be like this," I say.

We fall asleep, young and exhausted and covered in a smell I'm smelling for the first time. I think, this is enough. And it is, enough. No more, no less. Nice to be loved again. But not the reason I'm here.

The doctor told me how to jump. I could stay for the whole of a relationship, reliving each and every memory, until my time with that person was finished, until our body-to-body contact had been extinguished. Until the day and hour and minute of our last time. Then, I would no longer have a choice. I would be moved to the next whether I wanted it or not. *It is possible*, she said, *to get lost somewhere you did not intend to stay. Be wary where you linger. The memory is a clever trap.*

I jump from Anne to #2, that sharp pain between my legs. I lean my head back against my pillow, arch my back, do everything I'm supposed to do. I don't feel the explosive tremor through my body. I don't fake it, not yet jaded enough to pretend at satisfaction.

"Look, we're fucking," Mario says, enamored and amazed.

"No shit," I say.

Then I'm onto #3 with his clumsy drunk fingers. It's nice to see Daniel half-sane again. It's also painful, to see a ghost I finished mourning over two decades ago.

It's disorienting, jumping from place to place like this.

I land at #4. But this time it's different. I'm in a dark room in a foreign house, a place I long ago blocked out of my memory. I'm standing at the foot of a bed while another version of me pushes at the body in bed with her.

"I'm so tired," she says to the half-stranger, the man I have tried to forget.

I intended to jump immediately on from this one, to leave this room so quickly my eyes wouldn't even have time to adjust. But this isn't what the others have been like. I'm frozen by the sight of this other me.

I don't think about the fact that these are just memories, that the me in the bed is in no danger because it isn't real. I scramble up onto the bed and push the guy out of the way, pull my own body out of the blankets and then out of the room, down the hallway, onto his freshly manicured lawn.

He doesn't follow us. He's too drunk, almost as bad off as we are. It's no excuse, but it's the truth.

"Who are you?" the other me slurs.

"I'm here to help you. You have to get the fuck away from that guy."

"He wouldn't listen to me," she says.

"You should leave," I say.

"I'm too drunk to drive. My keys are in the house still." The other me rummages through her pockets and comes up empty-handed. I look for my car until I find it in the driveway, my old black sports car, beautiful and sleek and a piece of shit even then.

"Wait here," I say.

I sneak inside, back into his room. The asshole's passed out, mouth open, splayed across the bed. I grab my keys off the floor. I grab my favorite necklace from where it was slung across the room. I draw a cock on the back of his neck where he might not notice it for a good long while. It's the best quick revenge I can think of.

"I'll drive you," I say to myself. Already I feel myself slipping, feel the ground falling out from underneath me. When we get to the car, the ground is translucent underneath me. "Fuck," I say. I reach out and grab hold of myself. "Don't let go," I say.

And as fast as a sunrise when you're not expecting it, we're at #5, both versions of me, entwined with Natalie in a mess of limbs and tongues.

"You're so hot," Natalie moans. "You're both so fucking hot."

I untangle myself and struggle from the bed. The other me moves to-and-fro, too drunk to realize her deer-in-headlights expression is still pasted over her face. Natalie kisses her across her shoulders, across her neck, across the bridge of her nose and cheeks.

Natalie laughs, then falls away. "I needed that," she says. "I really did. You Pisces sure know how to make a girl come." She closes her eyes. "I'm glad you came over," she whispers as she drifts off to sleep.

I remember: we could never stay awake when we were together. Even the other me is falling into her own sleep, as unworried about her new location as I ever was in that time. I pull her from the bed and shake her awake.

"You have to stick with it," I say, leading her through the bedroom door into Natalie's living room, the floor strewn with astrology books and tarot cards. She had read my cards before we went to the bed; they were full of swords and cups, difficulties and loves.

"Where are we?" the other me says.

"We're safe here. She's wild but kind." I eye my camera sitting on her coffee table. I think about picking it up, but I'm already fucking with the memory enough so I leave it be, knowing I'll never see it again. "Just maybe don't leave your stuff here."

"I'm so tired." The other me clings to my shirt. "I can barely stand up. Can we go to sleep, please?"

I'm tired, too, so tired I can't make sense of the situation. I know I need to figure out what to do with the other me: what happens if I leave her in this memory? What happens if I keep taking her with me? Already, like faded scars, what remains of that night with #4 is falling away. The doctor did warn me, though I was too desperate to listen, that moving through memories might change them irrevocably. *But what really occurred, in your past,* she said, *that stays the same.*

This place is safer than most. Natalie won't mind if we sleep over. She won't wake in the night and demand anything of us. In the morning, we'll go out for crepes.

"You can sleep in there if you like," I say. "The bed is nice and comfortable. I'll take the couch."

"Thank you," she says. "Thank you."

She shuts the door behind her. I make sure the front is locked. I pick up some of the Natalie's things and stretch across the couch as best as I'm able. She has no extra blankets, so I pull a discarded coat over my body. I don't forget. I repeat the violinist's name again and again: Dover, Dover, Dover, until the lullaby of it pulls me under.

I RETURNED TO MY MEMORIES because I cannot live in my realities. People give many different reasons for going through with the procedure—to cure PTSD, to see a dead loved one a final time, because they think they can change things even though the doctors tell them they cannot—but they all boil down the same, don't they? They cannot live in their reality.

I, at least, was honest about this. The doctor appreciated my honesty, I think.

She didn't ask for much more than I put down on her paper. She didn't try to talk me out of it, which I'd heard of some doctors doing for patients without referrals.

I'm going to ride this all the way to the end. I am going to be in Dover's arms again. Because there was something in me then that she loved more than anything in the world. I need that back if I'm ever going to get her to talk to me again.

It's been three months since she last answered my calls. Three months is a long time to be without someone. Three months is too long to cling to old love.

Logically, I know this. But I dreamt about her every night. I remembered her every day.

To be bound to nostalgia, that's an illness deserving of a name, in need of a cure.

IN THE MORNING, MY OTHER self shakes me awake. I stare into her face, at her smooth skin free from sun spots, her unstained teeth. She doesn't look like she had a rough night. Sure, I had saved her from the worst of it, but shouldn't the very closeness to tragedy induce a fear of the world? Like the times I nearly but didn't wreck my car?

But yes, the time I did wreck it proved more difficult to forget.

"Morning, chip off the chipper block," I say. My back screams as I sit up. "Where's our lady friend?"

"She went to get pancakes," she says. "I like her a lot."

"Yeah," I say. "We did think we might be able to love her for a time, didn't we?"

"Can I ask you something?" she says, sitting at the foot of the couch only inches from my feet. "What are we doing here? What is this?" She runs her hands up and down her bare legs. "I don't feel right here. But, also, I love it."

I fold myself into the couch. "I do, too," I say. "Which means I should go. I need to go."

"So soon?" she says. "We just got here."

"We have somewhere else to be."

"Can we eat first?" She clutches her stomach. "I'm starving."

"You're not coming with me." I untuck myself and slip on my shoes.

"Of course I am! Where else would I go?"

"Stay here." My leather jacket, the one the memory me left on Natalie's floor, makes my skin itch beneath it. "You'll be happy here, for a while. Then you'll move along. And along again. And again and again." I grab up my old phone and check through the contacts, looking for the next in line. He isn't there yet. No matter. I don't need to call before moving to the first time we fucked; I'll already be there. I grin. He was good in bed, the redhead.

"I don't want that," she says. "I'm too tired for that. Can I come with you instead?"

Well, fuck. I can't leave myself where she doesn't want to be. She'll like the redhead. I'm sure she'll want to stay with him the way I always wanted to stay with him. After he stopped talking to me, I was sure my heart was broken, sure I'd had my first brush with near-loving a man.

"Come on then," I say. "Grab a snack bar from the kitchen." I watch the door. "If she comes back, we're never getting out of here alive."

Natalie was always aggressive with her goodbyes: those hard, knee-numbing kisses against the cold wall a memory I used to call up when fucking long-term partners, remembering the excitement of being wanted with such authority.

We disappear as the door's handle rattles. The noise becomes the knock of my head against the wood of a dresser, Christopher pushing into me from above. I grip his pink skin and moan. He doesn't notice that my head's hitting his dresser, softly but audibly, and this, too, is a turn-on: sex so rough it hurts. I'll walk the next morning on throbbing legs.

The other me, this time, is sitting at Christopher's computer desk. She's clicking through his music. My timelines, somehow, are crossing; this is what I would do after sex sometimes. The redhead introduced me to Bob Dylan, to the Band, to a hundred other all-male bands. He was never concerned with feminism; his house was woman-free except for me. I got a pass because I talked about women with the worst of them. Because I won games of beer pong too. Because I didn't ask to change the channel from football. (Though I should have; I hated football even then.)

"I've never heard of any of this music," she says. I think she's talking to me, but I can't be bothered about music right now.

"Hush," I say from beneath him. "You have no idea how much I missed this."

After he's come, he holds me and tickles me and kisses my neck until my skin is so sensitive, I beg him to stop.

"You've never heard of Bob Dylan?" he says to the me at the computer. "What have you been doing with your life?"

He puts on an album: *The Freewheelin'*.

"Play 'Don't Think Twice,'" I say with a hint of malice, though in all seriousness it's the only one of Dylan's songs that ever meant something deeper to me. I remember the redhead burning the CD for me, putting it on as I drove away from his house one morning. How beautiful was Dylan's pain! Then, later, it became the album I put on to commune with the ghost of Christopher's lost affection. I took a Bob Dylan class my second semester at college. Turns out he was a terrible sexist.

"This is beautiful," she says to Christopher. He beams and kisses the top of her head, like she's his fucking sister.

"This is Dylan!" Such excitement. I forgot how much of a fan he was, how much he loved the things he loved, how far I always was from being one of those things.

But when he crawls back in bed with me, I stick my hand in his red curls and smell the sweet toxic sweat-weed smell of his oversized sweater.

"He's cute," she says. "What happens with him?"

"We both want the same thing," I say, "But he talks me into wanting something more. And then decides against it."

He nuzzles his head in my lap. "Who are you talking to?" he says. "You're missing the best parts of the album."

"I'm talking to myself," I say, and both versions of myself laugh at the terrible joke.

WE STICK AROUND WITH THE redhead for another fuck. After that we drive back to my dorm room. When I pulled her out of her timeline, she had just moved in, and I wanted her to see the mess living alone became in a brief time. I'd written the address to a party on the wall in red paint. I'd been painting cartoons on canvas, love stories I was trying to make sense of: me as a mermaid, Pisces in literalization, with the Virgo sunlight-first-love pulling me from the water, saving me from drowning. A giant Alice holding on to the stem of a mushroom with a candy cane.

"Drugs?" she says. "We promised we would never do drugs."

"Weed is a drug, believe it or not," I say. "If you remember correctly, we also said we would never do dudes."

"That's fair." She picks up my copy of *Moby Dick*. "You're still not done with this?"

"I'm done," I say. "I'm twenty years older than you. If I can say I accomplished anything in life, it's that I read *Moby Dick*."

The other me slides into my desk chair. "Twenty years?"

"Resist the temptation to ask me questions," I say.

"Why are you doing this?" she asks. "Are you going to leave me behind eventually?"

I kneel at her feet. "I'll pick a good one for you," I say. "But Dover is mine. I want her to myself. You'll understand once you get to her. It's better than first love. Better than flimsy fucks. Better than the guy in the Winnebago."

"Winnebago?" She wrinkles her nose.

"Remember that. Treasure him. Oh, and Meredith. Treasure both of them. You'll remember them vividly for the rest of your life."

She plugs her ears with her fingers. "No more," she says. "I trust you. If you have to leave me, leave me with Winnebago or Meredith. But no spoilers!"

"No spoilers, no questions," I say. We shake on it.

WHEN WE ARRIVE AT #7, the other me bursts out laughing.

"What is this room?" she says. On one wall he's hung a giant poster of a woman straddling a massive nugget of weed. "Fucking stoner dudes."

"It's good for a guy, isn't it?" Simon says, that infamous line.

The other me rolls her eyes and crosses her arms. "Now this is a poor decision. That other stuff? Small potatoes."

"Shut up," I say, pushing him away and moving from bed.

"You made fun of me," she says. "It's only fair."

"I made fun of both of us. This is every bit your decision as it is mine."

She shakes her head. "I don't think so. The others I got. This one? We're not even attracted to him. This one is a sad fuck, plain and simple. I don't like sad fucks."

"You think I do?"

"I think you can't help it. It's not always about joy for you."

"Jesus," I say. "When did you become so insightful?"

"I have the added advantage," she says, "of meeting the me I don't want to be."

Simon massages my shoulders with sweaty hands. "I can't believe I fucked a gay chick," he said.

"An entry for your journal," I say.

"Don't talk like that to him," she says, sliding down beside him. "He likes you, and that's the only thing he's guilty of."

I turn and kiss him, to be nice. "You were good," I say, "for a guy."

"At least you were truthful with him," she says of #8, Oliver the poet. "That's the best I can say about that shit show. I've never met a needier guy."

"They're needier than we thought they'd be, men," I say. "It takes some getting used to."

At #9, Xander, myself and I forget him and dance until we're so sweaty we look like sea monsters freshly risen from the ocean. We stand in the bathroom mirror and watch the sweat drip to the floor.

Though I let her have Xander when the night is through.

"This one is fun," I said. "No muss, no fuss."

She spots his blue hair in the crowd. "That's him?" She laughs. "Is he wearing makeup?"

"He always saves the last dance for you. Every club night. Go get it."

I wait in his living room with the rolling kids, their pupils black saucers swallowing the skies of their eyes. They pass me a tab. I pop it and lean back into the couch. Might as well go with the times. We pass a joint as the lights go blurry, and they talk about the blue-haired boy.

"He saved my life," says a teenage girl. I remember this happening; I was there, with her in the kitchen. She thought she'd had too many pills. He gave her water and food and calmed her down. *I like helping people*, he said when she was better again, the revelation lighting him up like a fucking Christmas tree of cliché.

But damn was he hot with his plastic bracelets up and down his arms. I liked to imagine him in class, raising his hand, the bracelets falling together down his arm.

When she comes out of the room, she's white as a Mud Flap. And I remember.

"Oh, shit," I say.

She goes red in the face. "That's the worst possible thing you could have said right now."

I laugh because I can't help it. Other me isn't me, exactly; somehow, pulling her away from #2 in his seedy bedroom with his seedy insistent hands changed her. I don't know if I like her more or less than me; she's not as bold but she laughs easier, as though she's merely revealing what was always there. When I laughed, at this point in my life—*which I did so often I was known for it in my circle of friends—it was to let the mania hide the depression.*

"Admit it," I say. "You kind of liked it."

"Well, I agreed to it, didn't I?" She pulls at my arm, and her touch sends shivers, that old familiar drug jolt. "Let's go, please. Xander's sweet, but I don't think I can bear to see him again after that."

"Wise girl," I say, ruffling her hair.

She shrinks away. "I am so not your child," she says, then stops in her tracks. "Wait, do we have—"

"That's for me to know," I say, "and for you to find out."

MEREDITH PUSHES US UP AGAINST *the wall of the club and kisses us hard on the mouth. She tastes like whiskey and smells like sweat. She doesn't know that we have a girlfriend sleeping back at home; the other me doesn't know either.*

We kiss her back, our breath leaving our body like whispers.

Out in the parking lot, I unlatch my bike from the post after mucking around with my combination. We walk the bike the mile back to the house we rent with two roommates: a boy we went to high school with and another best friend soon to be gone from our life.

In our bedroom, we come upon the sleeping girlfriend. The other me shoots me a look; it's Anne.

"What is she doing here?" she whispers.

I bend to watch her chest rise and fall. "We don't love her anymore," I say.

"Well, what is she doing in our bed then? Why did we kiss that girl? Why don't we love her?" She sits on the edge of the bed. Anne doesn't stir. We have an unspoken arrangement, Anne and me. We are in a holding pattern, scared to move too far away from what we've always known. We won't say girlfriend but we will cuddle every night between the hours of two AM and ten AM. In the morning, her best friend and subsequent platonic life partner will knock on our door, let himself in. They will breakfast in my kitchen: eggs and sausage and almonds. They will ride their bike into the sun and will not stop riding until their legs are so sore, they can barely stand. She has sores from her bike seat. She has come a long way from when I first knew her, and I have come a different way, and there is no meeting place on our path except for in those brief eight hours when we sleep.

"This is no way to love," I say to myself. "We're too different now."

"Yeah," the other me says, "but it's nice to have someone to share your bed with every night. Someone who cares about you."

"We're happier without her," I say. "Remember the good stuff, sure, but don't forget that there's a reason we broke up in the first place."

"I remember. I was there the first time around." She reaches up to touch a necklace that isn't there. She will still miss him, Daniel, in a way that is not strictly platonic, strictly the grief of losing a long-time friend to a black hole of illness. She will not have changed her number yet. He will call her for years, will make her wish she could close herself up. I forgot, but I saved her from all that, too. When he slipped his necklace around our neck: "I never want to see anyone hurt you." But his was the greatest hurt of all, unintentional. I still startle when I think I see him in a crowd.

"There were other reasons we broke up," I say. "Daniel was a convenient excuse."

We wake Anne. She holds us both. "You said you loved me," I whisper so low she can't hear. "But it was all gone at this point, wasn't it?"

She kisses me on all four cheeks. "Go to sleep," she says. "It's too late for talking."

I press my fingers to my lips where I can still feel a buzz from Meredith's kiss.

"Enjoy this part," I say to the other me. "That girl we saw tonight? She's going to change our world. She's going to be our friend for a long time. We'll stay for the duration of this one, I think. I could use a little waking up."

RELIVED MEMORIES PASS LIKE THE regular kind: hazy and over too fast. Here we are having a breakfast of granola with our very first love. Anne. Here, at a friend's party where Meredith, the cutest girl we've ever met, offers us greens on every bowl.

"I'm sort of seeing someone," I say.

"Me, too," Meredith says. "Some dude. He lives here, too."

Meredith and I don't kiss again until that night, too drunk to think straight, when she follows me home from a party. I remember walking. I remember telling myself to let her sleep on the mattress in the other room. I don't remember grabbing her by the hand and pulling her toward the empty bedroom. I don't have to remember it this time, because I'm here again. I don't drink as much but I make the same choice. The other me stands helpless on the other side of the room.

Again? she mouths at me. She tries to tug me back, whispers, *we're not a cheater.* But how does the saying go? Once and always.

Meredith pulls my tights half-off and buries herself between my legs and it's been so damn long since I felt anything fresh for anyone—sweat goes stale after too long on the body, and sunshine dims each evening—that I grip my hair tight in my hands and pull as hard as I can, a punishment for love, for the fuck-up of fucking another woman while Anne sleeps soundly in the bedroom we've shared since her new girlfriend Cathryn and her roommate Dana started fucking. I'm repeating a cycle she can't escape from. It's inevitable that we will end and begin like this again and again. I need to cut the cycle open, like a goddamn bedbug cuts its mate.

I'm supposed to fall asleep here. I pretend. Meredith stops, says my name. Shakes me a little. Huffs. Then she kisses me on the mouth, on the cheek. She brings my arm down over her shoulders and curls into me.

"So fucking cute," she says. "I'm in some fucking trouble with you."

This time, in the morning, I'm standing with Anne as she screams at me. My sister and her husband are there to pick up some things from the garage.

"Drama drama drama," my sister says.

"We didn't do anything," I say. "I passed out drunk."

"Why are you lying?" the other me says, leaning down to gather my underwear from the floor where I must have kicked them off. Meredith is on her way out the door.

"It's the script," I say. "It's what I'm supposed to say."

She shrugs. "What difference does it make if it's verbatim?"

"Yeah, fucking right," says Anne. She leaves the house in a huff, skids out of the driveway in a haze of upturned gravel.

That night, I tell my friends I don't remember a thing. "You had sex," they say. "Meredith told us."

"Shit." I'm driving. I grip the steering wheel. "I'm such an asshole."

"You already knew that," the other me says.

At home, Anne waits for me. We're supposed to go to a party together, our first party in years. She's realized that we're not long for our love. She's begun to give me mementos from our past, to remind me that I was once hers and hers alone.

"Nothing happened?" she says.

"No," I say. "Apparently, something did happen. I'm sorry. I don't remember a thing. I must have blacked out."

We talk over things, the word *girlfriend*, what it means to share a bed with someone, whether the world will end at the next scheduled apocalypse. We agree to try this thing officially. The other me rolls her eyes.

"You said this part was fun," she says.

"It's beautiful," I say. "Everyone makes so many beautiful mistakes."

But each morning Anne leaves. She returns each night. She finds a new place. We move her in. Meredith hangs on by a thread. Sometimes, when we're all together, Meredith gets misty-eyed and abandons ship, texts me something sweet once she's gone.

I can't, I text back. I show the texts to Anne.

The other me throws her hands out. "This is already a shit show," she says. But she's starting to like Meredith. Sometimes they take shots of whiskey together and flirt on the couch.

Meredith, myself, and I stake trash bags to the grass outside, wet them down. We slip and slide. Anne watches from the sidelines, teases us all about acting like children. She mocks us when we drink too much. She doesn't like to dance.

Meredith storms out one night, but this time when she texts it's *I won't see you anymore*. I don't text her back. I know that she is serious. She doesn't say things without meaning them.

"This isn't working," I say to Anne.

"It's her, isn't it?" Anne says.

"Yes and no. We keep trying but it's just not there. You're not here. I'm not here."

"We're at different places," she says.

"This is absolutely the right decision," the other me says. "Third time's not quite the charm."

Anne pushes her. "I like her," she says. "She's not as worn as you. Is that because she hasn't fucked as many dudes?"

I purse my lips to keep from snarking back. Anne's hurt. Even as we say goodbye, I'm itching for Meredith's soft lips, for that leer that means I'm in for it. For those vulnerable nights when Meredith tells me, back turned, about depression. How it's a thin word that will break if you push it too hard.

I call Meredith as soon as Anne leaves.

"I'm moving to Colorado in November," Meredith whispers one night. That means we have four months, and it makes it sweeter, that end-date staring at us from the future. Meredith holds both of me. We imagine the day she'll go. We feel comfortable with permanence as long as it's temporary. We imagine ourselves kissing her as she loads herself into her car, our face wet and our voices strained at goodbye. We write a poem and call it "November."

A month into our relationship, I pull Meredith into the kitchen and tell her that I love her because I know she wants to hear it and I can't stop thinking about her. She flirts with other people, and I don't care because they're just words and looks and it doesn't impede what we have. She accuses me at every turn of loving other people.

But it's her and her only. It's her because she pulled me from a dangerous loop.

Then it's still one month until our scheduled end, her move to Colorado, and I catch her with Cathryn. Meredith admits to it straightaway as we stand in the rain outside my house, hoodies up. The other me stands beside me. I tell Meredith to go.

"I mean, look at how you got together," the other me says as we watch Meredith walk away down the sidewalk of our backyard.

"It's not her leaving that gets to me," I say.

"Then what is it?"

I shrug. "I'm hurt," I say, "but it's because she ruined what would have been a beautiful ending. She's just a confused girl. She's so young."

"Not much younger than you."

I shake my head. "No, she is," I say. "She'll grow up. But right now, she's young and scared, and I wouldn't have known how to help her. It's good that she's going. I only wish she would have taken a different route."

But down my back yard there is only one sidewalk. She pauses at the fence and looks back at me, her hoodie obscuring her red cheeks.

"Did we really love her?" The other me presses her hands against her chest, as though to warm her heart. "I can't tell."

"It's hard," I say. "I still don't know."

I grab hold of the other me's hand. There's only one path, and we've already traveled it.

NEXT THING, WE'RE IN A garage apartment on Halloween. Across from us sits a butch woman in a Chick Magnet costume. We kiss her. We fade. Short and sweet.

"THIS NEXT THING," I SAY to the other me, "is something you may not understand."

We're in a room lit by the orange string of lights strung around its ceiling. Anne's old roommate, Dana, stands naked at the foot of the mattress on the floor. She slaps a ruler against her open palm: Do you measure up? the ruler reads.

"Kiss her," Dana says, motioning to Cathryn, Anne's ex, the woman Meredith fucked. I kiss Cathryn. The other me furrows her eyebrow, pulls me away. Cathryn kisses Dana, the timid woman turned dominatrix-lite while I follow myself into the bathroom.

"What the fuck is this?" the other me says.

"I don't know," I say. "It's revenge. It's everything coming full circle."

"It's ugly," she says. "It's wrong."

"No, there's something beautiful in this," I say. "It's not immediate on the surface, but it's a method of forgiveness."

"Maybe sex shouldn't be a vessel for forgiveness."

"Sex can be whatever it needs to be. Sex can be whatever you want it to be. Sex can be nothing, even, if you play it right."

I jerk away from myself. "You can't judge things when you haven't seen the whole story. You'll see. You'll know eventually. Sex isn't about love all the time every time."

She lets go and crosses her arms. "Shouldn't it be?" she says, and I can't tell if she's telling or asking.

I shrug. "We're not exactly the same people," I say. "I can't answer that for you."

"Is this fun for you?" she says.

I think back, to the first time, the second time, the third time I slept with these two. A mess of memories. I thought, for a moment, I might find a routine with them both. But then the painful truth crept in: I wanted to forge my own path. If monogamy wasn't for me, I wanted to find that on my own terms.

I never once thought monogamy wasn't for me with Dover.

The truth of those threesomes with Cathryn and Dana: I wanted Dana, the woman who had never fucked me over, who had never slept with two of my exes, but in order to have sex with her, I had to have sex with Cathryn, too. They were a matched pair even if Cathryn cheated on her. I was acutely aware that Cathryn was both superior and inferior to me simultaneously. That women chose to be with me in the light and her in the dark. That women got from her what they couldn't get from me.

"It's not particularly fun," I say to myself. "But you never know if you don't try."

One thing I was always proud of: I knew what I really needed, and maybe I tried to need something different, maybe I tried many things, but I was always honest, in the end, with myself.

"I guess," she says. "I'm so tired. Doesn't this get tiring?"

She's still the relationship one. The one who wants a promise before the naked glimpse.

I remember not-sleeping. I remember crying until my cheeks burned. I remember lying on my wood floor and playing the same song over and over. Heartbreak is terrible and wonderful and numbing, and I missed it when I was stable.

"It's hard," I say.

"Then why not stop?"

"Because it's all hard. Not just this. Everything. Being alive," I say. "It's hard, but it's what you know and so you go with it. Go with it."

"I'll go with it," she says. "If it seems like something worth going with."

I peek out the door. She's right; I didn't enjoy this night, or the night after, or the night after. I wanted complicated and I got complicated.

I grab her hand. "You're right," I say, and we're on to the next.

HUNTER, THEN, THE GOOD POET, the artist, his Winnebago full of canvas and fast-food wrappers. The other me scowls when she sees the mess, but then he kisses her, us, and her frown is gone. This, then, is a threesome she can get behind.

He's the first man to give me an orgasm. When we leave his Winnebago in the morning, we find nothing more than my bike out front. We wheel it down the busy stretch of road back to our place.

"It's too bad he's not for us,' she says.

"It's fun with him at first," I say. "Then not anymore."

My muscles ache. My mind's numb, not just my body. I'm tired, just as I said I would be at the last stop.

"I need a break," I say. "You were right. This is the part where I need to be by myself."

"Let's do that then," she says. "Let's be by ourselves."

WE SPEND THE WEEK WE would have been with Hunter writing, reading. We don't go to class; what's the point, when we'll only have to leave again and forget all we learned about Physical Anthropology and Statistics. We spend evenings with friends who will later move away.

One night I buy a gram of weed and place it into a metal tin. FOR DOVER, I write on it. FROM YOUR SECRET ADMIRER. We drive by her house and leave it on her doorstep. She might think it's creepy. She'll probably think it's a prank being played by her friends. But she'll smoke it nonetheless.

I try to see her through the front window, but there's no one home.

At home I show the other me her picture on Facebook. "This is it," I say. "This is her. Maybe you can do it different, when you get there. Maybe you can keep from fucking it up."

She tries to smile. "If I'm you," she says, "doesn't that mean we'll make the same mistakes?"

This is where I said I would leave her. But I don't want to let her go. I stay a little longer.

We go to the astronomy center for their monthly star party. We lay on a blanket and name the constellations. She remembers many that I can no longer name. I know only a few she hasn't yet learned.

"What do we do, in the future?" she asks.

"It's a surprise," I say. I can't tell her about the numerous shitty desk jobs, the two years of cleaning houses, writing essays on the side, in stolen hours, losing friends to make time, trimming the fat to make time. No more painting. No more running. Until we catch a break: one book deal, then two, then a third. Dover's celebratory dances. Then the stress. Then the disappointment that success did not fill the void. Then a man, one who made me feel, once more, wanted. Then the need for a wreckage that would move the rock blocking me from more, from new ideas. A stalemate of a house. Another advance, this one enough to pay for the procedure but no more than the one trip through.

AT THE END OF OUR week, myself and I are watching a movie on my old beat-up couch, and I get a phone call from a guy who was in one of my classes, someone I used to buy weed from and flirt with when there wasn't anyone else in the picture. The tattooed misfit. Jeremiah asks me over. I look over at the woman who is both me and notme. She won't like this one: no-emotions, hardly even a kiss between us.

I try to hold on, but I feel us slipping into his apartment. And if we don't, if I let us keep ourselves from going there, we won't get to our final destination.

Because I don't want to shield her from the ugliness that is sex with the wrong people—because I want to instill in her that regrets will not ruin us—I keep us there long enough that she can see our mistake, long enough that she can look him in his face, then go. Go again. Go again. Go again. Jeremiah and Michael and Michel and Grayson and Eliot.

"What are you doing?" she asks. "Who are these people?"

"They're the low before the high," I say.

When we wake up in Eliot's strange bed, our memories wiped by too much booze, I look over at my own wounded and confused face.

Eliot drives us home. He jokes about herpes.

"This guy's a real asshole," the other me says.

I sit with her on our couch. "He is," I say. "But Dover is next."

"As long as you know." She crosses her arms. "I don't trust your taste at all. What if I don't like Dover?"

I shrug. "You won't," I say, "at first." I grab her hand.

"Are you ready?"

She looks so scared and so rundown that I hardly recognize her. I think of the past few years: years of rundown and scared, scared of everything. How Dover must have seen that in me day after day and still loved me. How Dover loved me even after I fucked someone else. How she insisted we stay together, work it out. How I couldn't look at her anymore. How it was me who walked out the door and made her realize that she could live without me.

"Let's go," I say, and then we're off. We're in Dover's bedroom. We're kissing. As innocent as fools. Dover's lips are beautiful and terrible, a reminder I wanted nothing more than to have. Her glasses hit mine and her violinist hands tangle themselves in my hair and she is a different person. I am a different person. The other me watches, her hand at her chest. I imagine the other me is stricken with a feeling like remembering something you never knew.

I push my finger against Dover's lips. She gives me a goofy grin. It doesn't suit her, too drunken, her weed-eyes half-closed.

Dover doesn't love me yet. I don't love her yet. When we first meet someone, we cannot love them. As we remain in one another's company, we absorb pieces of the other: a party trick. Only once we are part of this other person, only once they are part us, can we love them. Narcissism at its best. It will take us six months to amalgamate.

I look over at the other me. I step out of the bed. Dover's room is a mess of dirt and dirty clothes: failed gardening experiments and the slovenliness that comes from college living. She's cute like a child is cute. So is the other me. I miss the Dover who loved me, the one who stood by me through disappointment, the one I held when she needed it. But that Dover isn't mine to kiss anymore. I've spent a long time trying to get back someone who isn't here. I wrap my arms around my other self. Her heart hammers.

"Don't leave," she says. But I let go and jump before she can stop me.

"No thanks," I say to the next man, unwrapping myself from him. I'm alone, the other me still in that world-before-the-fall. "I've got to get home." I climb out of his bed. I fall into the dark. This time it catches me.

The doctor waits with me until I wake. She hands me a box of juice and a cracker. It has been less than six hours since I went in. She checks her watch as I drag the juice box straw across my lips.

"Was it worth it?" she asks as I sit up in her chair. She hands me the paperwork to take to the front desk, sign. There's no price on it, as though numbers don't exist, as though to trick me into forgetting what I've done until I emerge from the fog. There will be a number later: delivered to my mailbox.

"Is it ever?" I say.

I walk home, too drowsy to drive. I pick up my phone and dial Dover's number. Her voicemail picks up, as it always does when I call these days.

"I'd be lying if I said I didn't want anything from you," I say. "I want you to hear this and come running back. But I'm not going to ask it. I'll do what you requested. I'll leave you alone now. I only needed to say, because I don't think I ever did, not really, not without bending it in the hopes that it would pull you back. I'm sorry I cheated on you. That mistake was on me. I hope you're happy where you are. I hope you're safe. I hope you can forget the good parts enough to move on. I hope—"

The voicemail cuts me off. I stand in the desolate street and stare at the bright screen.

Press 2 to start over, the phone says.

I press 2. I hang up. I walk home.

I CAN'T ESCAPE MY JOB. Everywhere I go, I see ads for the company. On the subway, the sidewalks with our company logo engraved in concrete, the talking billboards which feature the intertwined bodies of flawless men and women in the downtown AdZones. I'm good at what I do. PlayMatez look and feel real: warm skin, a clean but undeniably human smell. Only "real" isn't a word we're supposed to use. Of course, they feel real. They are real. What I mean is they feel the same as blood-and-guts people do. They walk, talk, and fuck the same.

Except for the damaged ones.

The damaged eat with their hands. They'll eat whatever you give them—stale cornbread, powdered milk, reconstituted beef cutlets—and demand nothing more. They wear this far-off expression whenever they're addressed, as if they're calculating the benefits of an answer. When the damaged speak, they speak in near riddles which I have always suspected have no solutions.

I work in the building where they make PlayMatez, both the damaged and the ones that work right. It's a fifty-story skyscraper on the edge of the industrial district, which looks like most every other district, shiny buildings packed tight as the pedestrians rushing down grimy sidewalks. Except in the industrial district, smog fills the streets from a ten-hour flow of traffic, the constant hum of machinery operating inside. Our factory is one in a long line of unidentifiable factories, all black. In the basement, human and robotic workers toil over the assemblies. I've been down there only twice. The workers' bodies are all bone and bulk; our robots are constructed from bioengineered human muscle. That and Cyberskin, our own patented silicone/skin blend. The only way you could tell the humans from the robots would be to look at their insides. It's my job to know what those look like. I build the internal networks, sculpt intestine from tubing. My work is replicated by the millions.

My workshop on the third floor is concrete and steel. Outside the door is a silver plaque with my name in bold letters: ROBIN UNDERWOOD. The inside has a window on which I've hung purple curtains to make the place seem homey. In the hazy daylight, I carve muscle tissue with a sculpting knife. I bend microfilaments into circulatory shapes. I work alone, hunched over a table that lines the whole back wall of the workshop, and shape the parts I'm given until they look satisfactory. Then I ease them down into the plastic PlayMate mold to make sure they're the right size.

Once I've got all the parts in there, save the upper muscle layer, I often stop and stare. Inside the mold, thin, green wires reach like a hand into the head, crisscross through the torso and down into the arms, the legs. They don't carry blood through the body—our PlayMatez are bloodless—but they do carry heat. The handbook says when the wires have been activated, they glow blue like veins. Some of the organs we don't bother with. The ones that filter waste are useless, as any food consumed travels through the pink intestinal tubing intact and exits as it would in a human, but whole. The ability to eat is just for show. Once I'm done gaping, I lay down the final muscle layer and weave the wires through it.

The table's been organized into stations, a new station for each part, except the skin and bone. Another woman works the skin. The tech for these parts isn't mine. It filters down from the fiftieth floor. All I do is figure out new ways to make it fit, new ways to make the robots more authentic. I also sculpt hearts.

But for every hundred PlayMatez that come out normal, one comes out wrong. It's a glitch in the system, and like clockwork it occurs at the same intervals.

The damaged have cold skin, a malfunction in the wires. And like I said, something weird in the expression, in the way they speak.

The damaged aren't sold with the rest. They're sold, the females and males alike, to specialty shops, bulk buyers. Management knows what those buyers do to them. We ignore their beckoning fingers when we pass them on street corners in less favorable parts of town, in which the majority of us factory workers live. I can't be seen picking those damaged up. The ones I collect come from the subway, where they cower in corners and eat the skin off rats. Even though they don't need to eat, they've been programmed to. There's a switch in the control panel that lets you turn that off, but most people are scared to touch them, and in the subway it's hard to tell the damaged from the homeless. I know them because I'm drawn to them.

THE FIRST WAS A DAMIEN II. He carried the name on his inner thigh, and when I lifted the edge of his shorts in the half light of my apartment to find it, he slapped my hand away.

"What's black and white and cheeky?" he said.

"I don't know. What?" I asked, but he just laughed. He was strange-looking, beautiful of course. They were all beautiful. But his beauty, unlike the other Damien IIs, was forced. He shouldn't have been beautiful. He was too broken for beauty. I'd found him wandering the streets like a lost child. He couldn't have been older than three, though of course he was built to resemble a twenty-five-year-old. His model had been released five years previous, and it was still in production, though soon to be retired. The Damien II's bulky body had light features, light skin and eyes and hair, and he was prone to fits of giddiness. In the damaged that giddiness manifested as an inability to be clever, his riddles repetitions of the same template.

"What's white and purple and sunshine?" he said.

"Are you hungry, Damien? Would you like some pasta?"

He nodded. I fixed him pasta from a can. As he ate each string of spaghetti, picking it up with the tips of his fingernails and dropping it into his open mouth, he looked not at his plate but off into the darkened bedroom across the apartment.

I had little experience with the damaged then, one on one. I asked him if he saw something. He didn't answer until his plate was empty, the pool of tomato sauce at the bottom untouched.

"If the blind can't lead the blind, who will they turn to?" For a moment his lips were a narrow line. Then he broke into a blank grin. "What's white and white and white all over?"

He was, white all over. When he took off his clothes, even his nipples were so light they glowed in the dark. I liked his whiteness. It kept me at a distance from memories I would have rather forgotten but which loomed in the brute thrust of every man, human or not: the memory of a dark and warm body beside me, the bitter smell of oil paint and turpentine heavy in black patches of body hair.

Instead of curses the Damien II moaned nonsense, words pulled from his language bank seemingly at random: stripes, dartboard, keel, burst. Any neighbors listening in wouldn't have had a clue as to what we were doing. I wasn't worried about people listening. They were too absorbed in the constant hum of YouChannels.

As he slept, I imagined what his wires looked like, that blue glow inside him. I wondered what his breath looked like leaving the lungs I had made. How his skin would come apart to reveal my masterwork. I traced a line down his back and pretended my finger was a knife.

I KEPT DAMIEN II FOR six days, until I began to worry that whoever owned him, and he was too clean to be abandoned, would come looking. It was theft, after all, of the highest class, as PlayMatez were valued not only monetarily but also emotionally, as precious companions. And he wasn't what I was looking for, not really. I wanted one whose riddles made me shiver. Like the painter used to, when he sketched me with my clothes on and made me feel like he was painting the invisible pieces I could never show him. Words that would open me up and leave my insides exposed. Without that, I couldn't be bothered to take care of someone. But when I found it, I told myself I would hold their hand and keep them safe even as they self-destructed. Which was inevitable with the damaged. They wore their riddles out until they could no longer form words or even master the complicated muscle movements of a smile. I'll be honest; I wanted to watch. I wanted to be there for their destruction. It intrigued and repulsed me.

I wasn't allowed to buy a PlayMate for myself. Conflict of interest: we signed a contract. If we were to grow attached to one of our own creations, it might affect our decisions. We would be tempted to change things we wanted to see changed, to create models we wanted, not models that the public wanted.

Instead, we cared nothing for the models we worked on. Each worker was in charge of such a small portion of the product that it was easy to be detached.

Following my week with the Damien II, I took home as many damaged as I could find. None of them were what I was looking for. I brought back a Ken V, an original Matthew, even a Max II, trying to wrap my head around what it was I wanted. They were crazy, of course, but their riddles were often monotonous, the same old tricks of language. Uninspired. Random. The Max II even seemed to have a hold on where he was, what he was. His riddles were nothing like riddles.

"I'll take care of you, my Clementine," he said, leading me back, down, into my bed. "I'll make the ceiling spin like roses."

After I let them free, I watched them wander off into the world again, back to their subway stations or the homes where no one watched over them. I wasn't sad to see them go. Some, I knew, had probably been shoved into closets, deemed broken, only to escape when their switches were turned on by some nosy kid. If I knew they had no one to go home to, I opened the control panel in the upper left side of their chest, passed over the red dials and the memory slot, and switched off their hunger.

The truth is I don't know where they went when I let them go and I don't know where they came from before I picked them up off the ground or carried them from the dumpsters. I cleaned them. Always I ran water in the bath and let them soak, wiped the grime from their faces, from their bruised bodies, not like a mother but a cold stranger doing them a cold favor. I gave them clean clothes, that once belonged to the painter; he had left them. In his clothes, the damaged seemed as if they could walk into our factory and earn their own keep. The regular ones could do that, of course. That's what happened to most of them after they were no longer wanted. They could earn their price back and be given a life of their own. But not the damaged. They can never work.

THAT'S WHAT I TOLD MYSELF when I finally did cut one open, that he would be helpless and alone in the world. I tried not to look at his name when I did it. I just wanted to see inside. My fingers itched for it. When he was fast asleep, naked, on his stomach in my bed, I took a knife from the kitchen and ran it down his back, right where I knew the seam had been. I peeled the skin back as little as I could manage while still being able to see inside. I figured it would hurt less, opening the old seam wound. Because these PlayMatez, they feel pain. They feel it at smaller doses, but they feel it nonetheless. That is part of what makes them so believable.

Inside, the wires I crafted gleamed blue in the light that crept through my window from the streetlights outside. It is never dark in the city. I could see the wires embedded in the thick red muscle tissue.

I opened the flap wider, so I could take in all of the upper back. I wanted to know if my handiwork was what had made him damaged, but everything else looked as I'd seen it before. I moved the muscles aside so I could see the deeper organs. He was a newer model, though not the newest, so his wires were a little thick, his lungs the color of vomit. I'd since fixed both of these problems, though peering in at the heart I noticed something I hadn't yet changed, something I had yet to even know needed changing: the heart pulsed on its own, a movement independent of its beats. I watched the red tissue bump bump, then pulse, bump bump, then pulse, bump bump, then pulse. It was expending more energy than it should with those extra pulses, pointless energy. The pulses weren't affecting his body in any way.

I touched the heart. It felt like a wet sponge beneath my finger. It was partly made of sponge. From far away it would have resembled a human heart, though it was a simpler design, a pear-shaped lump with a single opening at the top where the wires connected for the energy to feed through. Suddenly he moaned, and his insides shuddered. I panicked. Pulled my hands out of him and tried to shut his skin back, but I didn't have the tools. I backed away. He moved on the bed. I couldn't watch him stand. If he stood, parts of him might have bulged out the back; the spine, attached to the skin with the rest of his bones, wouldn't keep him from collapsing. I hesitated, stepped forward, then reached back inside and grabbed a handful of wires, tugging them. They sparked in my hands, then faded. His heart slowed, stopped, its final pulse even and sure.

I heard the sound of his machinery dying and then he lay unmoving on my bed. I removed the wires and spread them over the blanket and looked down into them. That was how I knew them best. Free of skin.

His body I tossed into the dumpster outside wrapped in a black trash bag. It felt like a dirty cliche, and even though I knew there's no crime against disabling them, I felt like I would get caught. That night I didn't sleep. Instead, I thought of that damaged I would watch destroy himself. I wondered if I really wanted to see someone else doing what I'd done to myself when I let the painter leave. But the idea felt too perceptive, and so I shook it off.

THE HEART TROUBLED ME. I didn't understand why it should be working overtime. When my shift was over, I went to the subway station. I found a young man cowed into a corner with several of the females, sleeping, dirt streaked across his face. A brand new model. So new the ads hadn't even gone up yet, and I marveled at how quickly he'd wound up here.

I shook him awake, took his hand. The strangers in the station probably thought I was a shelter woman, so I tried to act like one. I patted his hand while we walked.

"Oh, dearie," I said. "We'll have you fixed up in no time. Get that hunger switch turned off. Clean you up. Make sure you have a nice bed, yes sir."

Nobody looked me in the eye. What those ladies at the shelters do isn't thought of as a charity but a burden, one people didn't want to share. But of course, I reminded myself, I don't work at the shelter. I work for the company that put him here.

Back at home, once the Christopher had stripped to his skin, I ran the bath water and led him to it. I scrubbed all signs of dirt away, wondering how he could have gathered so much in so little time. It'd only been one month since we produced his prototype. He must've been one of three hundred models, tops.

Which meant there were roughly two more like him, damaged, out there already.

"I'm sweet sugar in my beginning, a rose in my middle, a sweetheart in my end. What am I?" he said as I helped him out of the bath. His flaccid penis slapped against his inner thigh.

"Oh, God," I said, laughing. "They sure gave you something to brag about."

There had been a push for a sensitive model. I imagined that was where his riddle came from, some combination of all the love words they programmed into him. It bored me. I wanted something that made a garbled kind of profound sense, something I might read in a poem, if I read poems.

I didn't let him dress. I put him into bed. Beside him my real heart raced. When I heard his sleep breath, deep and rattled, I cut him down the back.

He was so new his wires glistened. The heart, the newest model, pulsed the same as the other. I reached in and wrapped my hand around it. I ignored the movement of his body. I ripped the heart out. Ripped the wires. Piled them in a bunch on the bed. The body was silent, still. I hid the heart in the drawer of my bedside table. I sat and stared at the confusion of veins. My handiwork. I never could've imagined it would look so beautiful. Still it glowed blue with life.

I did this again and again, the next night and the next. It began to feel like part of a routine. Without it, without the dying embers of artificial life beside me, I found I couldn't sleep.

THEN I NOTICED SOMETHING DIFFERENT. He was an older model, one of the oldest, and when I pulled out his heart, it had begun to crack. I could see inside the complicated mess something I didn't make: a barely perceptible flesh-colored box. I removed it, and between my fingers the box squished.

It was a tiny rectangle, like a coffin for a cockroach, made of some material I'd never seen before, nearly transparent and near the same consistency of the silicone skin. There was something hard inside.

I dug my nails into the box, and the flesh stuff came away easily enough. I imagined that with a few more years of energy pumping around it, the box would have worn away on its own. I couldn't imagine how it had already held up for so long. Once I had peeled that part off, I held in my hands a hard metal screw, no bigger than my pinkie and rusted brown. I turned it over in my fingers. It smelled like wet copper. I lifted it to my mouth and stuck out my tongue. It tasted like blood—definitely copper.

I didn't understand. Why was it there?

I tore through my apartment, collecting all the hearts I'd saved from the bedside drawer, from my cupboard, from the bottom of the fridge. I tore each one open, and inside all of them I found the box. In some it was less worn, harder to tear, and in others it was more so. I collected the screws in a pile and stared at them, wondering. I wondered until my eyes ached. And then I slept.

I dreamt about wires wrapping around me. The wires crept up and over me from beneath the bed. I couldn't breathe they wrapped so tight, like a lover's desperate embrace. I woke up choking.

I TOOK ONE OF THE screws to work with me, and every ten minutes reached into my pocket to touch it, just to make sure it was still there. I wanted to know more. But there was no way to figure it out on my own. I would have had to give myself away. Tell them what I'd been doing. I would have to come clean. I could've lost my job. Without my job, I'd have nothing.

I went home. But not before I found another PlayMate to take with me.

His name, his thigh told me, was Lachlan 1.0. He was a middle-aged model, made back when the company was attempting to modernize its image. That soon went the wayside when they realized people wanted to be taken out of this world, put into a classic world they had only read about. Lachlan 1.0 didn't test well. He was updated to the Lance I not long after his design. They'd released the ones they'd already manufactured, but he sold poorly.

It wasn't just the name. The Lachlan was modern all over. He had metallic hair, cut into a Sidehawk. The hair on the one I found was greasy, flecked with dirt. All Lachlan models had an X molded into one of the front teeth, and a gauge in the ear so big you could fit a teacup in it, though the one I brought home had removed his piercing, leaving the shriveled hole. His model was thin, lanky, unlike the rest of the PlayMatez. Because of that, he fit in better with the young people. He could, the company had hoped, attract the large base of alternative youth, the only base we'd yet to conquer. As it turned out, the company didn't have a clue. They programmed him to say stupid things in an attempt at hip language. They programmed him to be impassioned about resistance to authority. They trained him to be everything people didn't want to see in a robot.

He did make a nice change to look at though. Across his upper torso, his living tattoo danced; comprised of microscopic LEDs, the ink ocean roared over his ribcage. His skin stretched tight over him like a canvas. When I gave him a towel, I was sorry to see him cover up.

I suggested we go to the bedroom, where I wanted to see his uniqueness prove artificial. On the inside, he'd look the same as all the others. He would have one of those screws in a box in his heart.

"Got any Pips?" he asked. He walked through the bathroom door and across the living area—my apartment was all open space in the common areas, no doors—into the kitchen. He searched through the cabinets which lined one wall.

He opened the fridge and studied the contents. "I dig a bowl of cereal in the night as well, if you don't mind."

Suddenly I was nervous. He was speaking like normal. But he had that damaged look, he did, and his voice sounded like an echo of what it should be, deep and lilting. He hadn't said a thing to me the whole way over, aside from some weird remark: "How does a train transfer someone from the underworld?" Now he was asking for Pips and cereal, neither of which I had.

And he had just let me bathe him like that. If he wasn't damaged, he should have objected. He should have made small talk, asked me my name.

"I have some whiskey," I said. "Old stuff. Just a bit left, but you can have it."

I pointed to the cabinet. He poured two glasses and handed one to me.

"Right well you do," he said as he took a sip. "This is rude stuff here."

I drank mine in a gulp. He refilled my glass.

"Lachlan, right?" I asked. "How are you feeling this evening?"

He still hadn't looked me in the eye. He peered into his glass, then across the cabinets.

"Better now, all cleaned off and all."

"Did you enjoy the bath?"

Then he did it, looked me straight on. "Right well I did." He winked.

I sunk into my dining chair. My hands trembled. I put my glass down.

"Didn't you?" he asked. "I thought that was the factual point." He stared back at the same spot on the cabinet.

"Are you looking for something?" I asked.

"You know I've been wondering, what's a rude woman like you doing, picking people off the streets? Honestly, I thought you were taking me to one of those safeties. Thought I was in for a feast. What you've got here is potato flakes and pastry cakes. Do you mind?" He took the box of pastry cakes from the cabinet, unwrapped one, shoved it in his mouth in one bite. "You're not exactly one of those women, are you?" he said, mouth full.

"I'm not," I said, picking at my nails. "Are you a cop? A representative of the company? Were you sent to make sure I'm not, you know, engaging myself with your lot?"

"Am I a cop?" He laughed. "Why, have you been unruly?"

"Of course not." I drained the second glass. "So, a representative?"

"You work for the company then? Right well. Methinks what you're doing here is unruly indeed, am I right?"

"All I've done is give you a bath, a bit of drink." I looked at the towel wrapped around his middle. "Would you like some clothes?"

He shrugged. "I imagine I'll be getting naked round here sometime. If I know your make."

"I didn't ask you here to get naked. Honestly, I was trying to help you. I thought you were damaged."

He grinned. His tooth was chipped below the X.

"I could be, if you wanted." He looked at me again. "What do women want?" He laughed. "That's riddle enough for the world. What is the square root of a woman?" He lifted the whiskey bottle and poured some down his throat. "What burns going down and sings coming up?"

"Stop it," I said. I looked at the door, then back at him. I crossed and uncrossed my legs, wrung my hands. "I was trying to help you. I didn't bring you here to mock me."

"I need your help," he said. "I've got all this energy. I need to know what makes a human hum."

When he moved toward me, I didn't try to turn away. He wasn't damaged, I could see that, not the way the others were. But there was something in him that was gone, and I wanted more than anything to find what it was. I wanted to cut him open anyway. I wanted to know what was going on in there. I wanted that body on my bed.

He pushed me past the dining table, through the door into the bedroom, onto the bed. Until, effortlessly, he was naked, and my skirt lay discarded on the floor. The warmth of his body startled me. I closed my eyes and imagined the painter. His skin the color of twilight. His sad brown eyes. But the painter had always been silent and steady when we made love, and Lachlan moaned and thrashed. Then came the awkward moment when I was done and told him, which set off his own spasm. They'd been made to trigger when we said so. He quivered under me.

Afterward I waited for him to fall asleep, but as the clock clicked past three in the morning he kept singing beside me, a vile drinking song.

"Don't you sleep?" I asked.

"Not much," he said. "Not if someone's eyeing me like that."

I tried to fake it, but the second my eyes shut, I was out.

WHEN I WOKE, HE HOVERED over me, a tangle of wires in his hands.

"I see why you were wigged," he said. "About me being a cop. You know, I don't think there's a law against this, though." He dropped the wires onto my bare stomach. "Except, of course, you work for the company. Can't own your own PlayMate. That makes this theft. And, to top that off, taking 'em apart like this makes it destruction of stolen property. The highest degree of destruction, methinks—artificial intelligence."

I sat up. Below him, covering the floor of my bedroom, were the rest of the wires I'd been saving, pulled from beneath the bed and strewn from the bed to the door. The drawers of my bedside table and dresser were open, wires spilling from them as well.

"No, you see, it's what I do. I sculpt those wires," I said, light-headed, heart stuttering.

"Right well. If you did, Ms. Robin Underwood, you'd know, wouldn't you, that the only way they color blue like this is from use."

"Of course," I said. "Of course, I know that. They were given to me, quite obviously, after they were dismantled. So I could look over my work."

"What I can't figure is, decent, rude woman like you, what are you doing snatching our insides out? What do you find in there?" he said, his voice hard.

"Are you going to go to the company? Are you going to tell them?" I could feel the sweat beads on my forehead. The room was hot. I tried to sit up, but I was too dizzy.

"I should. Save my own skin, right well?" Then, no warning, the blank look passed back over his face, like he'd never seen this room before. "But it wouldn't be like that. I would be wires and dirt, I would. Sure, they might fire you, but me— what to silence me but dirt?"

It sounded like poetry.

"No, I won't tell the company. Not if you tell me what you've lit on."

The words came easy. I wanted to explain, so he wouldn't tell, so he wouldn't think poorly of me, so he would understand, even just a little bit. I told him all of it, from the first uncertain reasons I brought the damaged PlayMatez home— that I liked the way my work looked alive and throbbing underneath me, and I needed something cold to hold onto, because a warm body would remind me of the painter, as his had—to my unbearable urge to look inside, to discover where a body's coldness came from. I told him of the discovery of the hearts' extraneous pulses, how I found the flesh-colored boxes with the screws inside. When I came to the end of my account, he looked at me as if I had told him I was dying.

"I feel myself running down, you know," he said. "Scares me right well. You know I'm not one of them, the damaged. But I've seen my make go that way. Most of the time, it doesn't happen soon enough. We're abandoned in closets and tossed in dumpsters." He gave me a look that, for a moment, made me question whether he hadn't been watching me all along, seen the trash bags I'd carried out. "But for those of us still switched on, most of us go damaged." He shrugged. ""Two to five years, if we're used proper."

"My work should last longer than that. It's designed to last longer."

"What of those screw boxes? How long they rigged to last?"

"I don't make those," I said. "I don't know where those come from."

"Methinks we're not rigged to last. Methinks permanent companionship, it fizzles out in five years tops."

"How old are you?"

"Five. And a half."

"You look good, for your age."

Up close, his eyes were as grey as the smog outside, his eyelashes long and beautiful. The dark must've kept me from noticing. Or maybe I kept me from noticing, unwilling to grow attached.

"I don't know about you," he said. "But I want to know what's inside me."

I shook my head. "I couldn't."

"Not that, you wacked woman. I want to go to work."

WE RODE THE SUBWAY OVER once the building closed. I had a key, for those late nights working, that would get us through the front door, but it would only get us as far as my workshop. Lachlan told me not to worry, and though I didn't know if I could trust him, I didn't care. I was tired; what we were doing made my stomach spin as it hadn't since the painter and I made silent love on the kitchen floor. I led Lachlan through the lobby, sneaking past the camera's gaze. We rode the elevator to the fiftieth floor. We exited. These were the doors that belonged to the people who did nothing with their hands. They watched and decided, but they'd never touched one of them, not in any professional sense.

Lachlan led the way. As it turned out, he'd been there before. He was, he admitted in a whisper, hired by the company. They'd seen me, didn't I think they would see me? In the subway, lifting the damaged from the ground, dragging them with me on the train.

He knew where they would keep the files.

I wanted this adventure. I wanted to run back home. I wanted to push Lachlan against the wall and take him. My breath shook. But I knew what we were going to find. Really this trip was just for show. I knew I'd lose my job, sooner or later, and Lachlan knew he'd lose himself. Of course, the company programmed our robots to fail. Of course, the boxes were meant to biodegrade, the screw to be let loose into the heart, where it would puncture and damage the tissue irreparably. Companies had been manufacturing products that would run down eventually for years. It started with refrigerators and now here we were.

But why were some of them made damaged? If the company created them on purpose, was it for people like me, too broken to keep unbroken things around? I half hoped this was the case. It would mean there were enough people like me to warrant a market for them.

Once we were by the office door, Lachlan wedged his fingernail into the skin on the right side of his chest and pried his control panel open. He pushed his finger into the panel and pulled out a square chip as small as a tooth. At first, I thought it was his memory card, but it wasn't. There was a slot in a similar panel next to the door, and he pushed the chip into it. The door clicked open. We went inside.

"How did you do that?" I asked.

"I saw them do this when we met here before, to complete my paperwork a few years ago. I recognized the tech. Rigged one up myself," he whispered, though we were alone. "Spiked the cameras, too."

The file cabinet was locked—the company kept their files stored on discs outside the computer, for fear of hackers, competitors, and free rights organizations. Lachlan picked it with a hair pin. I wanted to laugh, but I couldn't bring myself to make the noise. Inside he found several spherical discs, the size and shape of gold balls, labeled from the start of the company, twelve years ago. He dropped them into the bag he'd brought. We left the way we came in.

Afterward, as we ran through the streets, clutching the bag, I felt the air on my face, and it felt like it used to, when I was a kid, when I was a young woman in love with a flesh-and-blood man whose clothes were covering the body of the robot running before me. I had to stop several times to catch a breath. Lachlan ran ahead on thin legs.

The painter's legs had also been thin. Always he moved like a shadow through my apartment. He too was broken. "Depressed feels like such a thin word," he had said to me often in that dark, "and it's such a thin feeling." He passed that brokenness down to me. He had dreams of another country, of walking on green instead of grey. When he got his chance, he went.

"Come with me." We had been in bed. Outside we could hear the muffled roar of the billboards going in the AdZone four blocks down. A sound you got used to. He claimed he had never been used to it, never would be. "You need to get out of here."

"I can't," I said, rolling away. How could I go with no guarantee we would make it, no guarantee that life was better on the other side? His darkness was beautiful, but he would drown me in it in a world where I was nothing but his. After all, a place is just a place. There would be nothing there that could sculpt me into a different kind of person.

I didn't go with him. He left me behind.

At my apartment, Lachlan went through the files, plugging the discs into his panel. When he found what we were looking for, I brought it up on my computer. I was right and wrong; the damaged weren't a mistake. Or they weren't as big a mistake as the company would like people to think. They were, the files said, an unfortunate consequence of the built-in obsolescence, the biodegradable flesh-colored box, the screw that the company placed in the PlayMatez' hearts so they would wear down within five years or so, causing the customer to purchase replacements. Without the built-in obsolescence, the company's base of satisfied consumers would remain satisfied—there would be no reason for them to buy another PlayMate if their first continued to function—and the company would cease to turn a profit. Ten dollars extra it cost them, per model, to install the screw. Only in some models, the damaged, the body rejected the foreign object. It hadn't been programmed in and therefore wasn't part of the system as the electronics knew it. They were unable to function properly even the five years it would take for the screw to come loose.

Some might say, I thought as I read over the text, that the damaged are the smart ones. They know something's the matter with their parts, and they won't pretend it isn't.

"Robin, how could they know?" Lachlan asked, popping the disc out of the computer's drive. "How possibly?" He downed another Pips. The empty bottle clinked on the concrete floor where we sat, the discs strewn about us like marbles.

"I wouldn't know," I said. I felt like I should apologize to him. But I also felt as if he too must have known that this was what we would find, and so part of me thought he'd been searching for it all along.

"The factual question is, how do I get it out of me?"

There's no way, I wanted to say. Once the skin is open, there's no way back.

"We could broadcast this. Maybe, once people see ...." he said.

"Maybe," I said.

His eyes narrowed. "You think they already know."

My hand rested on his shoulder. His eyes lacked the lively dart of human eyes. When he spoke, people knew that the number of things he said was exhaustible; he had only so many possible combinations of letters and numerals, only so many inflections. His wires would burn out, and there would be no grave for him. There would be no graves for any of them. Their graves would be the junkyard, and when the record of our time was lost and all that remained was our bones, the damaged would have no names because they had no bones. Their parts would be melted down to make more things that people use to fill the empty spaces in their beds, their workrooms. I realized that Lachlan's skin was cold in my palm.

"We should tell them. We should try, at least."

There was a grin that I'd never seen on his face, wide-eyed and stupid. This, it seemed to say, was an entirely new kind of adventure. This could get us killed.

But I knew the truth: that he had watched too many movies on the YouChannels, too many thrillers where the consequences of corruption are always disastrous. I humored him, because I loved the grin. It reminded me of a grin I used to know. My own.

When we went to bed, he talked like he was on upper. As the night passed, his words warmed the room. I entered the space between dreams. His words made less sense.

"And then, of course, I said, why else would a door be like a cockatiel? And the chief said, cockatiels only take wing north in the evening. And I knew then of course, how could I not have, that the cockatiel was like a door in that it was also like a desk."

In my sleep I muttered, "What's a cockatiel?" It was a word I didn't know, and I was surprised he knew any word I didn't.

I waited for his answer, but all that came was silence. When I opened my eyes, he was gone. I wondered for a moment if I'd imagined him. Then I heard the noise in the bathroom, a clink, as if someone had dropped a pair of nail clippers into the sink.

I went to him. There was a window in the bathroom, and the street light shone across his naked body. I saw him barely lit in the mirror. His tattoo was glitching, the ocean seizing up. He stood at the sink, hands close to his face, and he appeared to be scraping something off the inner palm of his hand where his life line was. I was seized with the urge to know if his life line was truly as short as five years, tops, or if it stretched on, an illusion, if someone in the company thought of that; whether they made the line reflect the way things really were or the way customers think they would like them to be.

I stepped up close to him, so close I could smell his clean skin, the slight musk of his underarms. They did a good job with the smell. I wanted to see his lifeline. I wanted to help him wash away whatever mark had found its way to mar that line. But when I was close enough to touch him, I was close enough to see: a pair of scissors in the sink, a jagged hole the size of a button in his palm, and Lachlan tearing at the skin, pulling the wound bigger, until the whole of his palm was open.

I wanted to stop him, but I was caught by the beauty of that glowing blue wire in the dark, in the mirror. In his reflection, the light generated a shadow of his silhouette, but I couldn't focus on anything but how the beads of light blinked back at us in crisscrossing lines. They looked like elongated strands of the double helix.

"Am I a cockatiel?" he said. "Am I beautiful? Am I factual? Am I broken?"

These were riddles to which I had an answer.

"Am I beautiful?" he asked again. He looked into his damaged hand as the other hand grasped the wires inside. He tugged, and a wire snapped. His eyes in the mirror grew distant, colder than I'd seen them. I wrapped my arms around his chest and helped him pull the blue from his body. As we pulled, he wilted, until he was no more than synthetic skin and muscle on the floor. I peeled the skin away. I held his heart in my hands. The screw's pointed edge stuck out from the muscle, having finally worked its way through.

I never answered his riddles. The information I kept to myself, the discs I returned in a sealed baggie. I got out of that place, went to another city of grey where I got another job that followed me everywhere. I tried to avoid the cold. I left the damaged behind.

THE VILLAIN OF THIS STORY knew what it was to die. She died every day. Power down. Her vision a pinpoint, then nonexistent. This time was no different. The doctors took her pulse on the ER stretcher and pronounced her dead-on-arrival.

In the morgue, the villain of this story removed her face. She returned it to its owner, a woman who signed herself into the morgue under one of the villain's many names. The villain gave the woman a pill. The villain stayed with her and coached her through the fading light. "You'll be okay," she repeated to the woman. "I do this every day."

Once the woman was gone, the villain signed herself out. She left through the morgue's front doors. She let the cameras see her. They would not know her true face for the ghost it portrayed.

●◗

CAMILLE MAXWELL HAD ONE RULE: she didn't mix love and work. When her boyfriend Kingsley slunk into her office Monday morning with a ring box packed full of microscopic surveillance bugs, Camille shook her head.

"You know I don't do conflicts of interest," she said, snapping the ring box shut but sliding it into her desk drawer. "You'll win no favors from me."

Kingsley had dressed in Camille's favorite collared brown jacket and muted red sweater, the black jeans that hugged his legs. He sat in her client chair. "Please," he said. "I couldn't sleep last night. She's after me—I know it."

Camille Maxwell knew to whom he referred: a rich man's bogeywoman. All the tech CEOs discussed her in hushed voices at the poker nights Kingsley dragged Camille to once a month. Camille hated poker, but she loved taking Kingsley's friends for their money. After all, she needed it more than they did.

"She's not real," Camille said. "Your dumb friends are just bad people."

Robin Hood was a bogeywoman and a vast conspiracy. Over the last year, six tech firms had been sued to pieces by the families of various dead women. The women had all died in work accidents. The families had won each case, and online media was rife with takedowns of the powerful men whose lax safety standards cost people their lives. Instead of admitting that they didn't give two shits about their workers and were now paying for their callousness, Kingsley's friends had decided that the women were in league with one another, and that some other woman—Robin Hood—was the organizer behind it all.

Camille laughed. "I thought you were beyond all this. What made you change your mind?"

Kingsley reached into his pocket and pulled out a letter. He slid it across the desk. Camille picked it up. The return address seemed fake: Nottingham Lane. No name, but when Camille unfolded the letter from its envelope, she saw that the writer had indeed signed it *Robin Hood*.

They probably call you a nice guy. Maybe you really love the people you love. That girlfriend of yours—she must see something in you. She knows the you that's kept hidden from the rest of the world. Your parents probably love you. They're probably proud. You may look at yourself in the mirror every morning and think that if these people see something in you …. But I know you, Ralph Kingsley Gibson, beyond the secrets you keep from her. Beyond the face you show the world.

"This is clearly a prank," Camille said, but she didn't re-fold the letter. "Your so-called friends are messing with you."

"Maybe," Kingsley said. "Maybe not."

Camille had one rule. She'd broken it before, most notably when she had pushed the then-married billionaire against her old, unused filing cabinet. Camille had always struggled with tossing out old things. She cupped her hand between his legs. He sucked the breath from her. She hadn't been touched by anyone in a long time. Kingsley's friends accused her of wanting his money, but more than that, she wanted to remember that she was a person in the world capable of lust and, later, love. Kingsley was tender and rough in turns, and he had not spoken ill of his cheating wife even as he paid Camille to gather the evidence. *She needs someone who can give her more time than I give her,* he told Camille. *I don't blame her for that. But I need to protect my business in the divorce. People depend on me.* After they made each other come, they lay naked on the cold tile floor of Camille's office. Camille promised Kingsley that she would never depend on him. He had made no such promise in return.

"You know I don't do this," Camille said.

"You know you do," Kingsley said. "I'll pay you double what you'd ask someone off the street."

Camille sighed. She woke her computer. She opened her standard contract template and edited the numbers. She bounced it over to his phone.

"Sign it," she said. "Then we'll talk."

Kingsley leaned over to try to kiss her, but she moved her face so his lips landed against her cheek.

"I won't fuck you until it's finished," she said. "You'll just have to take comfort in one of those PlayMatez dolls or something. I'm sure Langston would cut you a serious deal."

"You and your rules," he said.

"Just sign the contract," she said. He smelled like a forest of artificial pine trees. It would be difficult to resist his body, but Camille was glad for an excuse to keep her from touching him. Her rules served one purpose, after all: to align the interests of her head with the itch of her heart.

THREE MONTHS PRIOR, WHEN CAMILLE first found Sadie Miller's lawsuit paperwork, she told herself she had not been snooping. She was not the kind of woman who should be invited into a lover's home. She made her living by sticking her nose where it didn't belong, and it was a habit that was hard to break.

As Camille read, she felt faint. An anger rose up from her belly to her throat. "What the fuck?" she said out loud. She pulled her scanner from her pocket and swiped it against the sensor on the underside of her arm: all levels normal. It was not internal, then, this rage. No rise in blood pressure. No surplus of testosterone. She read on.

She had not thought that Kingsley was a saint, far from it. But she hadn't thought that his misdeeds would feel so personal. It wasn't just that the ex-employee had sued Kingsley for the lung cancer she developed working on the car parts in his factory. It wasn't that he had hid the lawsuit from Camille; there was so much that the two hid from one another. It was the line at the bottom that got to her: *in addition to Ms. Miller's cancer, Ms. Miller has suffered from hormonal disturbances believed to be influenced by the proprietary chemical R used in your electric automobiles.*

Camille scanned herself again. She opened up her phone and looked at the detailed results: her own unbalanced hormones, the levels shifting wildly from month to month. She recalled the doctor who told her that no one knew why so many women were suffering, and maybe some unknown chemicals in our food or water was to blame.

She remembered telling Kingsley about the initial diagnosis, how she wished that companies would take better care to ensure that their products were safe for consumers. He had agreed with her, had assured her that consumer safety was one of his goals. There on the floor of Kingsley's bedroom, Camille laughed until she cried.

CAMILLE GOOGLED THE ADDRESS ON the letter Kingsley gave her. As she expected, the letter's writer had made it up. The writer had slipped the letter beneath the door of Kingsley's modern house right outside the city, no small feat considering his extensive security system. Camille had installed three cameras on his property and a doorbell that recorded all visitors. Camille logged into the security footage; the letter writer had cloaked themself in all black baggy clothes and a ski mask. They'd walked from some location down the road. Camille would find no answers in this footage, and when she searched her boyfriend's grounds for left behind clues, she came up empty-handed.

Kingsley watched her work from his porch. Camille had commanded him to stay there, and he was good at following her orders. Camille liked that about their sex life, but outside of the bedroom, she tried not to boss him around, even if he didn't seem to mind.

"She left nothing?" he said. "Not even a footprint?"

Camille shrugged. "Your grass is so fake, there's not a lot of places they could leave a trace."

"You still don't believe me," he said.

"I believe that your friends are some sick fucks," she said. She snapped a few more pictures of the yard with her phone. "Who'd you piss off?"

"You, apparently," he said.

"I rarely believe anyone." Camille slid her phone into her pocket. "I wouldn't take it personally."

"Would you like to come in?" Kingsley said.

"I've got a case to finish," she said, backing out of his yard to the driveway where she'd parked her old Kia with the manual locks. "Business before boyfriends."

"I'm ignoring the plural," he called out to her, but he was smiling. It was a game to him, like business, like that Susie Miller's life had been, like the lives of all the people who were not him.

WHEN SHE FIRST BEGAN, THE villain of this story searched the news for keywords like lawsuit, workplace injury, occupational cancer. She reached out to these women. Many of them turned her down. But then one would agree; they would give her their work badge, and their face.

The villain of this story went to the places those women worked. Outside the aim of security cameras, she set her fingers free; they scurried inside and left their own cameras behind. The villain of this story took the badge and the face and reported to work like it was any other day.

Coworkers rarely noticed. In the types of joyless workplaces run by people with too much money, people knew your name and the bare facts of your life, but the people you toiled beside ached in the body so badly they were unable to see into you the way you needed someone to see into you. The villain of this story made small talk. She laughed like the woman laughed. She looked like the woman looked.

If she bypassed questions posed by work friends, if she forgot the name of their dog, then it was because she was tired, so tired, and after all, everyone knew she'd been leaving work during lunch for those appointments.

The villain of this story sent something else inside with her cameras: a trap. As the machinery came crashing down upon her, she screamed the way the woman screamed.

● ●

IF CAMILLE WAS GOING TO take the case seriously, she would need to look into the cases Kingsley's friends claimed were enacted by the villain called Robin Hood. At least four of his friends had been victims, according to their poker stories, of workers' families suing them for deadly freak workplace accidents. Camille searched online for the cases, but most of them were hushed up to the best of the corporations' abilities. The articles claimed the cases had been settled out of court, the monetary sums provided to the families of the dead women unknown.

Camille made a lunch date with one of Kingsley's friends under Kingsley's name. She parked far away from the restaurant; she didn't want his friends to know her beyond what she chose to tell them. She slid into the seat across a small round table from Langston Eastwood. He looked up from the menu and frowned.

"Camille, what a surprise," he said. "Where's Kingsley?"

"It's just me, I'm afraid," she said. Langston had ordered two glasses of expensive French chardonnay. Camille took a sip.

"I don't understand," Langston said. "I'm not disappointed to see you, of course. But is Kingsley okay?"

"I'm investigating Robin Hood." It made her feel stupid to say it. "If I can prove her existence. If I can locate her. It would be helpful to you and yours, yes? I'm going to ask you to cooperate with me, and I'm going to hope that you choose to do so." The waiter appeared, and Camille paused to order. "More of this, please." She touched the rim of her glass. "And a blue dry-aged Kobe ribeye with the spot prawns, and cheese platter to start."

Langston smirked as he handed the waiter his menu. "I'll have the same, but make mine medium-rare." He clinked his wine glass against Camille's. "To hearty appetites."

"To rich dinner dates who believe in paying for a lady's meals," Camille said. "Now tell me about the case you think was orchestrated by Robin Hood."

IT HAPPENED LIKE THIS: A woman approached the villain of this story in a coffee shop. The villain of this story wasn't drinking coffee; she didn't drink coffee, didn't eat bagels, but it was built into her to desire the places her mother loved. The woman who approached the villain of this story wore a hospital bracelet and a curly-haired wig. The villain smelled on her what she smelled on the other women: desperation and death.

"I've tried to get them to pay for the chemo," the woman said. "But they refuse to admit that it's the factory's fault."

This part of the story was the same every time. The villain listened. She nodded. She patted the sick woman on the back. The woman was dying. The family would drown under the debt. The villain would make sure that didn't happen, would orchestrate a provable death, would find a way for the family to move forward with a clean slate.

The villain did her deeds: she unattached her fingers and sent them crawling. She installed her cameras. She planted her bugs. She went in the next day wearing the woman's face. She went to work supervising the assemblies. But it was not the same. Across the assembly belts, there weren't car parts or 3D-printed building materials or metal robot arms that would eventually be pieced together by a whole team of robots and their human supervisors. The assembly belt carried women with skin stretched across bodies that were part metal, part flesh, and they blinked at the villain as they rolled past, observant but silent, their voice boxes not yet activated. What had this woman's job been again? The villain paused. She was to inspect the teeth. She missed the first who rolled by, and the second. When the third came, she shook herself back into her body and stuck her fingers between the PlayMate's lips, pulled them back, and glanced at the teeth as the woman below her stared with furrowed brows at the villain, her inspector. How frightened she must be. How confused. For one moment, just one moment, the villain let her true face show. Then she recovered, remembered the mission, and became once more the woman who had numbed herself to this task.

OVER THE NEXT WEEK, CAMILLE Maxwell met with each of Kingsley's four friends over lunches for which they paid. She picked their lies from truth like crab meat from the shell. She asked for the security footage from the accidents as well as any extra footage the courts had provided; several of the women had recordings from their own cameras, a standard occurrence since the age of #metoo.

The results yielded no additional information. The workers had indeed suffered freak accidents; there was no denying it. Most of the factories in which these women worked hired humans to oversee the inexpensive robots they used for manual labor. Women were a popular choice; they cost less to employ than their male counterparts. The private footage was no different. Camille checked her levels as she worked. Two hours in, her blood sugar blinked low on her sensor. She went into her office kitchen for a glass of orange juice and a handful of peanuts.

When she returned, the autoplay had moved to the last factory's footage, the footage from Langston's place. Camille had saved it for the end. Langston's business creeped her out more than the others; he made people. They were mostly for erotic purposes. They were, she was told, the best of their kind: the PlayMatez brand. Torsos rolled across assembly belts in the background. The dead woman, the victim, strolled into the factory. She took her place at the inspection platform, changing shifts with the previous worker. They nodded to one another as they passed. She stopped as the first body rolled by. Then, there—a glitch in the video. Camille paused the recording.

It might have been imperceptible to someone unversed in deception, but to Camille the glitch stood out. She frowned. She rewound the feed. It glitched again. She opened up the official factory feed. It had a glitch in the same place. Camille logged into the Death+; she had an account from her few cases that involved suicides. It was a good place to look for morbid videos posted by people who accidentally caught footage. She searched through the posts tagged #factory. Sure enough, there it was; a woman from a prior shift had left her surveillance running. She'd caught the victim's death. And there, minutes before the accident, where the previous videos had glitched, was something strange: the victim's face changed.

The billionaires were right; there was a Robin Hood, only she was more involved in the process than even they had believed.

THE VILLAIN OF THIS STORY scrubbed the video feeds before returning the victim's footage and a backup of the factory's to the victim's family. She had been sloppy.

Her mother would have chastised her, punished her, but for the villain of this story, the mistake was intriguing. It was almost human, the reaction she had felt to the assembly line women who looked so much like she looked. She wished that she could help them—could save them from their programming. And yet she understood that she owed her existence to them, to the technology that had led to her own creation.

The villain's mother had once worked for PlayMatez. She had seen the factories, had worked for a man like Langston Eastwood. She had helped build the parts. The woman's name had been Robin, not Hood—that was silly, the fancy of men who likened themselves to kings of mythology—but Underwood. The thing was—the villain knew, when she went in to the factory, what she would see on those assembly lines. She understood in the most rational parts of her programming. But it had struck her anyway.

No one was immune to pain. No one was immune to mistakes.

CAMILLE GRINNED AT HER FINDING: a woman's face. Sometimes, when working a case, she had one of these moments when she felt certain of her success, when the path to truth became clear. She felt a lightness in her belly. On her screen, in the Death+ video, she was staring at the face of a woman who was not where she was supposed to be. Camille pulled the scanner from her pocket and took a reading; her blood sugar was dropping. She opened the bag of peanuts that she kept in her pocket and poured them all into her throat. Her body was needy today—hungry. She tossed the trash at the can and missed, but she didn't dare stop for the amount of time it would take for her to correct the missed aim. She snipped the photo of the woman's face. She plugged it into an image search. One result came back, an archive from the PlayMatez employee database: the woman's name was Robin Underwood.

EVERY TIME THAT THE VILLAIN of this story looked in a mirror, she saw her mother's face. Robin had built her in her image, like the most narcissistic of gods. Robin II, the villain called herself, though she did not ponder the implication that she was second to the woman who had been made fully of flesh, no plastic parts, no manufactured organs.

Robin II had been created for this one purpose: to ensure that fewer women suffered without recourse. Robin Underwood had intended, she told Robin II, to build more, to start a whole movement. But the maker had perished before she finished her creations. Occupational cancer, only Robin Underwood had not worked in the factory when she realized that she was sick. Robin II could not profit from her death. So Robin II did the work for which she built, woman by woman, and tried not to remember the grand promises that her mother had made even as, every day, Robin II wore her face.

ROBIN UNDERWOOD WAS DEAD. CAMILLE frowned at the online obituary. She had died of cancer five years previous.

Camille called Langston Eastwood. "Does the name Robin Underwood mean anything to you?"

"It's familiar," Langston said. "Hold up." His voice went far away, like she was on speaker. "Oh, yeah, she was a piece of work. Fired. Broke into headquarters and stole some files. Published them, if I recall correctly. It was only a small headache for us, but of course we had to file a restraining order."

"What files?" Camille said.

"Fancied herself a social justice warrior or something," he said. "She took some schematics on the dolls. Tried to make a big deal out of the forced obsolescence. Thought people would give a shit. But, of course, every appliance manufacturer has been doing that for a while."

"Appliance manufacturer," Camille muttered.

"I'm sorry, I didn't hear you," he said.

"Do you know how Robin died?"

"She died?" Langston said.

"Thanks for your time," Camille said. She dropped the phone onto her desk and scanned herself. She wished the anger had a bodily cause, something she could fix. She wished it didn't creep into her once an hour. She wished that she had a way to discharge it, a way to be free.

As soon as Kingsley opened his door, Camille jumped onto him, knowing that he was strong enough to hold her and dexterous enough to catch her.

"This is against the rules," he whispered, and she pressed her lips into his to shut him up.

He backed them to the wall and pressed her against it. She unlatched her legs and undid his belt. She slid his jeans off. She ducked down and around him and pushed him against the wall. She took him into her mouth. She moved on him like she wanted to swallow him whole. She did want to; she wanted to take a piece of him that he could never get back. When he came, she kept going until he pushed her away, shaking in his sensitivity. He offered to make her come, but that wasn't the point, was it? She didn't want to open up to him. He was a nice guy, like Robin Hood had said in the letter, but the world was full of nice guys who did terrible things.

When she went to his bathroom to wash him off her face, she planted one of her bugs. One of the ones he gave her. She had no real reason to do it. But maybe, just maybe, she would catch something useful.

It wasn't difficult to find the woman who had stolen Robin Underwood's face; she lived in the unused warehouse that Langston Eastwood's restraining order listed as one of her known addresses. The warehouse had been used, for a time, as an unofficial homeless shelter for the damaged PlayMatez, dolls whose programming malfunctioned. At first, the company didn't worry much about letting them roam the streets. Then, once Robin Underwood released the documentation, the company rounded up the damaged and scrapped them for parts. The warehouse was condemned by the city, but no one cared to clean it up; it had too much of a past for that.

Camille ducked under a damaged door. She made her way through the rubble. She found Robin II charging in a patch of sun that leaked through a broken window. She crouched beside the woman; there was only one way she could have stolen the face of Robin Underwood: she too was a doll.

"I know who you are," Camille said.

Robin II startled awake. "Don't turn me in," she said. "I just needed a place to sleep. I got kicked out of my housing a while back. You understand, don't you?"

"You're not human," Camille said.

"I'm just a homeless woman," Robin II said. "Please, they'll put me in jail."

"You're the one who's framing companies," Camille said. "All the women who have died in those accidents? They filed failed medical claims against the company first. All for occupational cancer. You helped them."

Robin II shook her head. "You've got the wrong person."

"I mean, I understand that they still died. They were so sick. But you helped their families."

Robin II struggled to her feet. She hovered over Camille, who continued to kneel. "Who are you? Why are you here?"

Camille pulled from her bag the papers she'd photocopied from Kingsley's files; the claims by the woman who had once sued him. "I want to help you help this woman."

Robin II took the papers. "Do you know her?"

Camille shook her head. "I don't."

Robin II folded the papers and pocketed them. "Do you know when they discovered that asbestos causes cancer?" Robin II asked. "1935. You'd think they would have had enough time to find something else to use when manufacturing their building materials and toys and, yes, precious cars." Robin II helped Camille to stand. "I know you. You're his girlfriend."

"I am," Camille said. "I have access to the homes of several other CEOs. I have expensive bugs. I can help you, too."

"What did he do to you?" Robin II asked.

"He loved me," Camille said. "He didn't do anything wrong."

Robin II thought a moment. She scanned her records for Camille's name, her face; she seemed trustworthy, and her digital footprint didn't contradict the original assessment. Robin II scanned the sensor tucked into the skin at the back of her arm; her blood pressure was not high, like a liar's might be, and Robin II understood through the hormonal composition of her body that she was hurting from the inside out. Even if the man loved her, he could not heal her from there.

"Why do you hate him?" Robin II said.

"Why did you write that letter?" Camille said.

"What letter?" Robin asked. "I didn't write any letter."

Camille's chest seized; Robin II felt Camille's heart palpitate. She had been right all along; the letter was a prank.

●●

Two weeks later, one of Kingsley's self-driving cars killed a woman crossing at the crosswalk. Camille didn't hear from Kingsley for a full week except when she listened in to the sound of his crying in his bathroom, until he showed up at her house with his bags packed.

"I'm moving on to a new venture," he said. "I'm stepping down from the company. It's what the investors want."

"Where are you going?" Camille said.

"For now? Florida. To begin training volunteers. We're going up, Camille. New World, Inc."

"Going up?" Camille looked at the sky. She groaned. It had been a long-shot dream of his for a while. "Space travel, you mean."

"Mars," he said. "Come with me. It's the future, Camille. It's a fresh start."

"This is the fucking future, Kingsley. I'm moving forward," she said. "Where you're going? That's the goddamn past."

When he went in to kiss her, she moved away. It didn't matter if there was a rule or not; she didn't want to touch him ever again. Later, she would read about the funding for his missions, how he claimed that Mars was a bi-partisan issue even as he accepted money exclusively from religious lobbies who longed to create their own non-secular societies. If she had gone with him, she would have been stuck in a world that didn't want her. Would he have even told her?

After he left, Camille opened the door to her guest bedroom. "He's gone," she told Robin II. "Gone for good."

Robin II lay across the bed that Camille had given her. Out of the darkness, she heard Camille's voice. It pulled on her. She rose to the surface of her body. She opened her eyes. She came back to life.

BEFORE SHE ENTERED KINGDOM ARTS, Camille Maxwell kissed her cyborg girlfriend goodbye. It wasn't an act of affection that her girlfriend needed, but they both liked the normalcy of kissing in their otherwise unusual lives. Camille scanned her sensor: her blood sugar levels were slightly elevated. She'd eaten a lunch of peanut butter, oatmeal, and a whole bag of carrots to compensate for the time during which she wouldn't be able to snack. Everything else read okay—she should be good. She'd have to be. She'd run out of medicine two weeks ago—and the money to replenish her stock. It was why she'd taken the billionaire's silly job. But virtual reality was safe, as long as she didn't spend too much time in there, as long as her heart rate didn't jump too high from adrenaline. It was unlikely, from a video game.

"If I don't make it out of this alive …." Camille said. She slipped the VR helmet over her face and felt the device's electrodes settle into her temples. The motorized strap whirred as it tightened.

"It's a job," Robin said, crossing her arms. "In a video game. Don't be dramatic. I'll be watching your levels, Camille."

Camille started to reply, but before she could, she felt herself falling through the floor of her apartment. The smell of dried feces and wet rock overwhelmed her. She gagged as she struggled to find her footing then realized that her feet had been planted firmly on a rock floor all along. Shadows surrounded her, and as her eyes adjusted to the low light, she saw that the shadows were shapes: a woman with her arms curved above her head like a ballerina; several ducks with long necks; a man holding a bow and arrow. Their features solidified until they were the shapes their shadows represented, two-dimensional but undeniably real. The dancing woman lowered her arms.

"You're here," she said, her voice scratchy and deep, as though she had not spoken for years. "You're here to help us."

"I was hired to help you, yes," Camille said. She studied her own body; it too was two-dimensional, a shadow come to life. In the background, the words MAGURA CAVE etched themselves in the air then faded as tribal music swelled.

"Our creators were some of the first," the woman said.

The man lowered his bow and stepped toward Camille. "We are some of the first creations."

The ducks quacked. Camille furrowed her brow. "Right, I'm here to help."

"It is time," the man boomed. "We must gather!"

All around, shadows chanted and moved. Firelight rose from the air and cast upon the woman. She grew taller, wider, and she bent and scooped Camille up into her massive palm. Camille lost her balance and fell onto the woman's skin. She wrapped her hand around the woman's thumb as the woman lifted Camille. The woman's giant face appeared in front of Camille.

"In your pocket, you will find the invitations. Deliver these to the leaders of each world. We must meet at the end. You must get these messages to everyone! You are here to help! So, help!"

The woman heaved her hand up and sent Camille flying. Camille landed on hands and knees upon another surface; she studied the lines of the new palm. She was in another hand. That hand passed her to the next hand. She scrambled up fingers, fell through the gaps between. She felt the heat of sweaty palms. Faint auras formed around the hands: red and brown and golden yellow. She crawled from hand to hand, and upon one of the hands, she read a tattoo: CUEVA DE LAS MANOS.

Camille paused, remembering herself, and sighed. It was all a game. She couldn't let herself forget. She took a deep breath and played, making her way through the labyrinth of hands, until the hand she settled upon shone gold as her feet touched its surface. She stopped. The hand inflated like a balloon beneath her until she was not standing on a disembodied hand at all but the upturned palm of a golden statue. She peered up at the statue's face: it was the face of Zeus.

ZEUS AT OLYMPIA appeared as a reflection in the gold of his crown.

"What do you think so far?" Zeus said.

"I'm here to help," Camille said. "To deliver invitations. I suppose you're supposed to receive one?"

"Camille," the statue said. "This is Ashton Moore. It's called an avatar."

Camille struggled to her feet to face her current employer. "I thought you'd be meeting me at the beginning."

Zeus smiled, his ivory lips cracking as they upturned. "I wanted to give you some idea of the immersion!"

"It's great," Camille said, forcing her voice to show some degree of excitement. "Really something."

"You're our first beta!" he said. "I mean, that's not what you're here for, but still. We're very happy to have you. I work on each game for years without any feedback. And then, something like this happens—and it just kills me that I may lose everything—" Zeus began to clench his fist, but Camille cried out before he'd closed his fingers over her completely. "Sorry," he said. "It's infuriating."

"I can only imagine," Camille said. She crawled onto the statue's wrist. Better safe than sorry.

"Oh! Wait!" Zeus said. "There's this brilliant feature where if you enter my orifices, you get to relive many of Zeus' adventures."

"I'm not here to have fun," Camille said.

"No, quite right," Zeus said. "But you'll need to play through to access the trouble spots. You need to see for yourself. The first one is inside my mouth."

"Good to know," Camille said. "Hopefully you've brushed your teeth today."

Zeus cackled, and as he did, his chest cracked with the force of his laughter. "I knew we hired the right person. They tried to warn me about you, but I knew better."

They meant her ex-boyfriend, who ran in the same billionaire circles as VR Guru Ashton Moore. Camille shrugged off the mention of him.

"Thanks for the opportunity," she said. "I'll get to the bottom of this."

"We'll check back later," Zeus said, and as he shut his lips, the cracks in his chest closed up, and the light left his eyes, and he was a statue once again.

EVER SINCE CAMILLE HAD EXPOSED her ex-boyfriend for the lax safety standards of his factory and his self-driving cars, causing his company's board to force his resignation, ever since she'd also exposed the lax safety standards of the factories of his billionaire friends, Camille had not been hired by many rich people. They banded together, the money hoarders of the world, and Camille Maxwell had no idea who they were hiring now to do the important work of trailing suspected adulterers and pothead teenage sons. When Ashton Moore had come into her office two weeks ago, she'd reached for the Taser she kept strapped to the underside of her desk.

"Someone has gotten access and is ruining my new game," Ashton said. "See, it's a new type of game-building. I'm writing the code from the inside! But someone has gotten ahold of a log-in. We've only seen their avatars, and they keep putting in elements that are not supposed to be there. I need to root them out."

Camille didn't ask too many questions about why Ashton trusted her when all of his friends did not; she didn't bring up the topic of her previous work with the too-rich. Instead, she bumped a contract into Ashton Moore's custom communications device—the weird rectangle he carried around could not be called a phone—and asked him to sign before they spoke further, for his benefit.

"I don't want any discussion of your IP without my being bound to an NDA," she said. "It's for your protection."

Ashton didn't read the exorbitant fee schedule before signing; he pressed his thumbprint to the signature line and bumped the contract back to Camille. Camille held in her exuberance as she talked through the details of the case: she would enter the game and try to suss out the identity of the hackers. Ashton told her very little about the gameplay, only that the game was called Kingdom Arts, an art history adventure.

"I'm making a case for virtual reality as the dominant art form of our time," Ashton said.

"I'm sure it's genius," Camille said. "I'll need the first deposit sent over by this afternoon."

As he bumped the money over to her, she slyly scanned her sensor, but the light-headedness was just excitement. She hadn't had a paycheck in a long while. She needed medicine. She needed electricity to charge Robin.

Ashton left the office, and Camille switched off the lights; no use paying for electricity for herself alone.

●●

CAMILLE CLIMBED INSIDE ZEUS' MOUTH. His tongue below her felt and smelled like a dirty sponge. Camille held her breath as she traversed the landscape of his throat. She scowled, then picked up the pace. She'd do anything to end the experience. She looked up at the roof of his mouth, its ridges and folds, and shuddered. At the end of his tongue, she found herself slipping down his throat. When she landed in his hot mess of stomach acid, she expected to burn, but instead, she planted her palms upon a rocking ship manned by a woman in a feathered helmet with a spear at her side. The woman held a dead fly to her cheeks and wept over the creature's still wings.

The woman looked up, startled, but did not drop the fly. "I am Athena, daughter of Metis."

"How did you get this boat in here?" Camille said.

"I built it from my father's bones and colored it with the berries he consumed," she said.

Camille peered closer at the floor she still crouched upon; it was indeed strung from bones and smelled of rotting fruit. Camille tried to pick herself up, but the rocking of the boat made her unsteady on her feet.

"So far this game seems to be about bad balance," Camille said, gripping the side of the boat. She came to her knees.

"What do you mean?" Athena said, but at that moment, the sky opened up, and a man peered down the throat of Zeus. Athena's body grew, and Camille took hold of the woman's spear before it was too late. Athena grabbed the spear and struck wildly at the exposed air. Camille closed her eyes and wrapped her legs around the weapon, glad for the pole fitness classes she had taken before Robin, before the pursuit of justice that took up all their time.

Athena sprang from Zeus' body, and when Camille opened her eyes again, she found herself clinging to the side of a courtroom pew. Around her, women sat enthralled with the proceedings. The scene flickered, like a glitch, as Athena gave her testimony from the witness stand. The lawyer, a woman with fire for hair and one human leg, one donkey leg beneath her black pencil skirt, paced as Athena spoke. Camille clenched her abs, trying to keep herself from fainting from the unsteadiness and the lack of solid scenery upon which to fix her gaze, but her head spun regardless.

"He ate my mother," Athena said. Unlike in the previous scenes, the sound in the courtroom skipped. "Her body! Here!" And Athena thrust forward her palm with the dead fly upon it. "She was pregnant with his child! And then he went on to marry someone else in no time at all."

"I have no further questions," the lawyer said. She half-galloped back to the prosecution's table, joining a crowned woman in long robes.

The scene jumped, and the witness stand was suddenly empty. Camille searched the room for Athena, but she was nowhere to be found.

"For his crimes against women," the judge said, standing, "I sentence Zeus to execution! He will be turned into a cow and eaten!" She struck her gavel against her stand.

Zeus, in his gold and ivory glory, stood proud behind his defendant's table as two satyrs cuffed him and led him through a door.

"And yet we extol him and the art featuring him." The judge shook her head. "I do not understand it."

The glitch lines melted and pooled on the floor, and like wax, the courtroom melted to reveal a gladiatorial arena. Camille stood at the gate with her hand on the lever.

"What the actual fuck?" she said, and a guard holding a mace laughed beside her.

"First day on the job?" he said.

Camille looked out across the arena. On the far side, a paper-thin Jesus hung on a green cross. He was closing his eyes, and as he concentrated, the blood seemed to travel back into his hands.

"Better let the old boy free," the guard said.

Camille scowled, but she did as the guard suggested; it's what she was here for, to play the game, to find the hacks. She was fairly certain that the last scene had been an unstable addition, and that this scene, as bonkers as it appeared, was a purposeful part of Kingdom Arts. The image quality was better, and the sounds came through loud and clear. She pushed down the lever and opened the gate.

Zeus stomped forward on his ivory feet. Jesus climbed down the cross and took his crown of thorns into his hands, holding it like a frisbee before him. When he approached the center of the arena, Camille saw that she had been right in her assessment: he was thin as parchment, made from parchment, in fact.

"What is this bullshit?" Camille said, but she recognized the Jesus even as THE QUEEN MARY PSALTER drew itself in the sand at Camille's feet.

"You have a dog in this fight?" the guard asked Camille.

Camille shoved her hands into her pockets. "Absolutely not." She felt the invitations there. "Wait, yes, maybe." She pulled them out and read two names that had populated on two of the invites: JESUS and ZEUS. Camille groaned. "I guess I do."

As Jesus balled his paper fist, his skin made a crumpling sound. Zeus' heavy feet left inch-deep holes in the arena dirt as he made his slow way toward his opponent. As they approached one another, Zeus swung his heavy hand, but Jesus' paper head blew back, Matrix-style, as he dodged.

Jesus raised his palm and passed it over the dirt. The floor split open, and Zeus slipped into the cleft.

Camille jogged into the battle. She was thankful not to be on her knees, as so much of this job had required. She laughed at that; with a cyborg for a girlfriend, on her knees was not a place she often found herself.

"Hey, boys," she said, standing to the sidelines as Zeus clawed his way from the canyon Jesus had opened. "Stop fighting a minute, will you?"

The two deities didn't even look her way. "Isn't there some kind of cheat code for this damn game?" Camille stepped forward. The battle didn't smell like sweat, not the way a real battle would have, but like dust and gunpowder and the slightest hint of burning paper. Warmed up, the men attacked one another in a frenzy of paper airplane fist and stone strength. Camille tried to distract them again, to no avail.

"Rock versus paper," she said, then laughed at her stupidity, or was it the game's stupidity? She grabbed hold of Jesus' hand, and he folded into her arms. With one fell swoop, she covered Zeus' eyes with the parchment.

"I've got invites for you both," she said, and the two gods calmed, separated, and stood side by side.

"Who the hell are you?" Jesus said.

"She's been hanging around," Zeus said. He looked her up and down. "Shady, this one."

"Uh-huh." Camille passed out the two invites. "Don't be late." She wasn't sure why she said it, but as she did, the ground erupted all around them. It sprouted strange flowers that grew as tall as buildings, pink alien openings with golden petals encased in cracked-open blue orbs. Camille reached out to grab hold of Zeus' hand, anything to steady herself, but he was running into the distance, where a thin black sheet separated the landscape before Camille from a darker world full of black buildings and moving bodies Camille could barely see through the sheet. She looked to Jesus, but he had run off toward the left, where another black sheet hung; behind that one, blue mountains stretched, and animal sounds drifted. Camille staggered her stance and waited for the ground to stop moving. Water flooded up from the ground in the distance, forming three great pools, and then people fell from the crystal blue sky into a new soft grass. A woman walked by with a clamshell on her back. A man's legs moved out of the clamshell's opening. It was familiar to Camille.

"THE GARDEN OF EARTHLY DELIGHTS," the woman called out as she passed. "Get your earthly delights!"

Camille should have expected this. She waded through the orgy of bodies to the nearest pool and knelt. She splashed water onto her skin and let it travel down her face and drip into the ground. It was a delight, actually, and she studied the bodies engaged in a copulation handstand upon the rim of a giant blue globular fountain and laughed. Beside her, a mermaid android creature, skin as smooth as glass, dove in and out of the water. Robin would love that. Camille grinned. Someone threw a ball in her direction, and as she reached up to push it into the air, her hand sunk through the red, and red slid down her body until she was red from head to toe. She dove headfirst into the blue water, and the red washed off onto a scorpion with a hollow cavern instead of a head who swam to the edge of the lake and scuttled into the grass. Three naked men whooped and climbed inside the scorpion's cavern. Their butts shook as the scorpion waddled off.

Camille closed her eyes and let the water carry her on her back. The water was cool where it soaked through her clothes to her skin, and with no sun, only a blue sky absent of celestial bodies, the air was kind against her exposed face. What a game. Camille didn't play many of them, and fewer than that of the variety that required expensive VR headsets. She'd never delved into one of Ashton Moore's, but she understood that he was worshipped by geeks the world over for his eccentricity and his earnest ridiculousness. What had started as ironical fame had grown into stardom plain and simple. He'd made his fortune through surrealist sensibilities. Camille appreciated that about him even as she loathed him for his lifestyle. He wasn't as bad as her ex had been, but if she delved deep enough, she would likely find virtual skeletons in his closets.

Camille bumped up against a barrier. She opened her eyes: the black screen. She took a deep breath. She was probably meant to follow either Jesus or Zeus—she laughed at that—and she could not bear to see what Ashton Moore did with the ideas of Christian-centered art. She ducked under the black sheet and entered hell.

A black wall with open doors and windows lined the back wall of Camille's sightline. White light peered through, and Camille wondered where that light came from. The sky was black and grey, and the water was black and grey, and Camille crawled onto a shore of sand made of shadows. She looked to her left, where two disembodied ears wiggled side-by-side, a single blade stuck between them. People were trying to climb inside the ear canal, to escape, Camille supposed, for as she studied the people around her, she realized that many of them were not people at all.

The demons were in charge here. Camille walked as softly as she was able amidst the screams and hissing. A squat pink demon extended its tongue to write musical notes on a trapped man's ass. As he wrote, the music played; it was terrible, like the scratching of nails on a chalkboard, like the farthermost keys on a piano, like a pig crying before slaughter.

"It was my masterpiece," the man yelled, "and you're ruining it!"

Camille passed a bird eating a man while birds erupted from his ass with terrible popping sounds. She passed men hanging from blue glass and giant keys and knife edges pressed against shields. Camille frowned. Zeus was nowhere to be seen. The screaming intensified as a green dog-shaped demon ripped a man's arm from his body and tossed it to the ground. It landed at Camille's feet. Camille screamed as a spot of blood splashed onto her face. The green dog demons, who had been preoccupied with their meal, snapped their gazes toward her. They grinned terrible grins. They jumped, one by one, to the ground. They surrounded her. They sniffed the air. Camille smelled herself under her arms; she was ripe, which probably wouldn't help the situation.

"It's okay, I'm not real," she said, but the demons' only response was to growl.

Shadows moved. One of the dog demons collapsed. A sword poked out its once-growling mouth. Behind the demon stood a robust woman in a bright yellow dress with bellow sleeves. She yanked the sword from the demon's throat. Black blood poured over the ground and dripped from the sword point. The woman wore her hair in a braid atop her head. Beside her, a servant woman released the demon where she had pinned it to the ground. The other demons growled and dispersed.

Is everything all right? Camille heard her girlfriend say into her ear, outside the game. *Your heart rate is jumping all over the place.*

"Thank you," Camille said, stepping over the bloody lump. "I don't understand why no one gave me a sword."

Ah, there you are. Good, good. Camille smiled inwardly at her girlfriend's concern; her blood sugar tended to plunge with extended bouts of high heart rate, and stress made her hormones dysregulate.

"You're in danger here," the woman said.

"Well, yes, I had assumed." Camille waved her hand around. "On account of all the demons."

The demons flickered in and out of existence, and Camille's brow furrowed.

"No, because they don't like our kind here," the woman said. Her voice cut in and out. "My name is Judith. I murdered Holofernes." She gestured to the other woman. "This is my servant."

"Lovely," Camille said. "Congratulations on the murder." She needed to prod, to make the woman keep speaking, to figure out who she was, for whom she worked. "What do you mean, our kind?"

"Women," Judith said. Her servant nodded. Camille noted something strange about them: they both had their own arms, but they seemed to share a pair of legs, and they appeared to be leaning at all times, as if over a slain body. Camille saw, though she was sure she had never seen it at all, their source material in the back of her mind. It was an interesting feature, the insertion of art knowledge into her brain as she played, though she wondered at the privacy implications. She might mention that to Ashton when he asked for her thoughts. Or she might not. She needed to get paid, after all.

"Now, I believe you have a letter for me," Judith said.

"Do I?" Camille dug into her pocket. She pulled out the invites and searched the names. None of them were addressed to Judith. Camille frowned. Then she realized: Judith would have no invitation if she weren't part of the original game. Camille started to slide the invitations back into her pocket, but Judith snatched one.

"This one is mine," she said.

"But that one is for Adam." Camille snatched it back. She started to complain further, but Judith held up her sword, and Camille was struck with the sudden urge not to die. She shoved the invite into her pocket and ran. She ran as fast as she could until she hit the black screen that separated hell from earth. She ducked under the screen. A group of people had stuck their heads inside a pink flower. An owl nested on top. They danced around in a circle. Camille paused for only a moment. This place was ridiculous. She was ready to leave Bosch behind. The invite had been addressed to Adam. She recalled the triptych, the scene with Adam and Eve in the heavenly panel. She took a step forward, but she was too slow; from behind the screen, a hand closed around her upper arm and dragged her under. Judith hoisted Camille onto her back.

"Where are you taking me?" Camille yelled as Judith's servant used the sword to carve a hole in the ground.

"Where there are fewer places for you to hide," Judith said as the hole in the ground opened up, and Judith jumped through. They landed on a hill of green grass next to a dark blue river. VIEW OF TOLEDO, the dark blue clouds wrote in the densely clouded, turbulent sky. In the distance spread a city of grey stone. Though the setting's code seemed clean, Judith continued to glitch.

Camille groaned. There was nowhere for her to hide, not for miles, if miles were the unit of measurement for a world within a painting.

"But I didn't deliver the invite to Adam!" Camille said, angry that she wouldn't earn 100% completion in the game. She laughed at herself, at how quickly she'd become absorbed.

"We murdered Adam, too," Judith said. The wind whipped her hair around her head.

"Well, aren't you proud?" Camille said.

"It's my only sin," Judith said.

"Besides, you know, murder," Camille said.

The ground beneath them glitched, and Judith's servant tripped over a strip of static. The women separated. No longer of the same body.

"We have to hurry," Judith said. She bound through the grass. Her servant bound with her, and Camille felt as though she were riding through the landscape on the backs of two women, then one, then two, a blur of legs beneath her. Camille bounced against their shoulders.

At the edge of the city, they scaled the walls to a giant tower. Camille held on tight, afraid of falling, unsure how that would feel, how it would affect the gameplay. When they reached the top of the tower, they threw Camille into a window. In the middle of the room, sat a woman in a heavy white dress with gold and black accents. Gold lace covered her shoulders. Around her neck hung a gold beaded necklace, and a net of gold pearls held back her hair.

"I am ELANOR OF TOLEDO," the woman said, and her words formed bubbles that hung in the air then popped. "I have been expecting you!"

Judith and her servant cascaded over the windowsill and struggled to their feet.

"Who are you?" Elanor said. "I have *not* been expecting you! Guards!" Elanor reached up and pulled a rope that hung from the ceiling. Two men in armor rushed through a door hidden in the room's shadows.

"These women—this woman?—is here to steal my invitation!" Elanor cried.

Judith's servant somersaulted forward and, in one fell swoop, beheaded a guard. Camille screamed as it happened, but she was too late to look away as blood gushed from the empty neck. The servant tossed the sword back to Judith, who fought the other guard in a flurry of limbs. Elanor of Toledo fainted.

"How are you doing that?" Camille muttered to herself as she watched Judith fight.

"I'm broken as shit," Judith said. She punctured one guard through his chest plate. He collapsed to the ground. "Elanor, dear," Judith said. "We aren't here to kill you, but we do need you to come with us."

"She's unconscious," Camille said. "She can't hear you."

Judith hoisted the dead weight of the woman over her shoulders. Judith's servant bent to grab at Camille's legs, but Camille kicked her in the face. She fell back, then swept her legs around toward Camille's knees. Camille's legs buckled. She fell to the ground. Her head hit the hard earth. She disappeared into a haze like a blank canvas.

IT HAD BEEN A WHILE since Camille had been in real danger. Camille hadn't always cared about people. Sometimes, she still didn't care about them. She met Robin during her first big case, when together they took down Camille's ex-boyfriend. For Camille, the case had been revenge against a man who had lied to her. For Robin, it has been the pursuit of justice. After, they tried to take down a network of corrupt billionaires, to help the women who worked their factories destroy the higher-ups for the lifelong lung and other organ damage. For their troubles, Camille was served with a lawsuit and a search warrant of her apartment for reasons the officers did not make clear. Robin wasn't home at the time, thank goodness. If she had been, if the officers had figured out what she was, she would have been taken away from Camille. Robin's creator had worked for the world's largest manufacturer of cyborgs, and Robin was made of stolen parts, complete with serial numbers stamped into the most fragile parts of Robin's body.

Together, Camille and Robin agreed to pause their work until it was safer. Camille promised to vet each case for its risk to their lives. But Robin subsisted on justice and did not take part in pleasure for pleasure's sake. To do so would be to give in to the programming that had first plagued her parts, to backslide to the kind of consciousness that existed for fun and fun alone. Camille hadn't noticed Robin's sobriety when they'd been part of something bigger. But Robin's cool calculations of risk versus reward meant the couple did very little outside the comfort of their home, and Camille, who was once wild, missed the fearful beating of her own heart.

And then, there was the issue of medication. As long as there were no paychecks, Camille had no way to stabilize her levels should they become elevated. Robin understood this calculation, too, and scolded Camille when she went too long without a fibrous meal or skipped out on her daily, carefully planned workout.

That is to say, as Camille fell into blankness, she felt a feeling she had not experienced in some time: joy at not knowing where and when her vision might return.

When the game flickered back, Camille was once more in Hell. Only it wasn't the Hell of Bosch but the hell of some cheesy-looking horror film: a lab, glitching with her every breath. Judith and her servant bent over an operating table. They'd left Camille forgotten in the back of the room. Elanor slept beside her, still out cold. Camille stood and peered over the table. Her heart jumped into her chest. A man's naked stone body lay across the table, but his stone head had been severed and set at the table's edge. It peered out over the lab with unmoving eyes, a helmet with wings atop its curly hair. Judith's servant fired up the torch welder as Judith pried a stone Medusa head from the body's grasp. Judith held the head to the body's neckline as Judith's servant moved the flame. The glitches intensified as stone formed to stone.

Camille shook herself out of the torch's trance and searched the room for an exit. There was a single door on the room's far side, barely visible through the static. Camille slunk back to the ground. She crawled on hands and knees, trusting the distraction of the strange surgery. But she felt a hand upon her ankle.

"I have to get to the gathering!" Elanor said. "You have to help me."

"I don't," Camille said, then remembered: she wasn't here to help any of these characters. She was here to save the game, to find out who was behind the hacks. And in this room, she had two characters created by them. She shook free from Elanor's grip and stood once more. "What in the hell are you two doing?"

Judith jumped, but her servant held the torch steady.

"Making improvements," Judith said. Her servant turned off the torch, and Judith stepped back. "See? Isn't this better?"

Medusa's head was welded on Perseus' body. As Camille approached the revised statue, Perseus' severed head spoke: PERSEUS, he said, and blood leaked from the place where Medusa's head had been attached to his old body. WITH THE HEAD OF MEDUSA, the blood spelled as it formed a necklace around her new neck, lagging all the while. Medusa opened her eyes. She grinned a terrible grin, and the snakes of her hair struggled to life.

"You're taking elements of the game and changing them," Camille said. "What's the point?"

Judith and her servant placed their hands underneath Medusa's body and lifted her, light-as-a-feather, off the table. Medusa looked wildly about but could not move the stone of her arms. Judith's servant approached Elanor on the floor and captured the noble woman's hands behind her back. "Stand," Judith said. "Look at the beast we've made for you."

Judith's servant forced Elanor to stand. Elanor did as she was told; she looked right into Medusa's eyes even as Camille tried to warn her against it. As Elanor made eye contact, the stone melted from Medusa's body and crackled up Elanor's until Elanor's stunned expression was frozen in time. Medusa stretched her new flesh fingers. She flexed her new arms, rippling Perseus' muscles. She lurched forward on stiff knees. She raised the sword still clutched in Perseus' hand. She thrust it forward toward Judith's servant. It slid through her and ripped her body like a canvas. She fell to the floor. Judith called out, but Camille grabbed Judith and pulled her toward the door. She yanked at her frozen body, not frozen in stone but frozen in fear or grief. Judith finally followed.

The door led to a blank room. Camille shut the door behind her and leaned, panting, against it.

"What is going on?" she said. "Why didn't you just kill Elanor if that was your intention?"

Judith groaned. "It wasn't supposed to go that way."

"Then what way was it supposed to go?"

"We're not in the business of murdering women," Judith said.

"What in the hell do you mean by that?" Camille said. "You're in the business of murdering other people?"

A redhead stepped out of the shadows. "Don't believe a word they say." She wore her wavy hair down her shortsleeve red dress, one side pinned back with a barrette. "They'd murder me in a minute. What am I if not a woman?"

Judith groaned. "You think you're so clever, Mr. Moore," she said. "You're not clever."

A man in a blue suit and grey fedora stepped out after her. "I am clever," he said. He winked as he grabbed hold of Judith's arm and the woman grabbed hold of Camille's. "Watch this."

The floor opened up like a trapdoor, and the four of them fell through a tunnel surrounded by bright green code. Judith mumbled, *lousy NIGHTHAWKS*, and her words formed words in the code, and then they landed upon a pile of bodies, some of them naked, others clothed in rags, bloodied and bandaged, black and white. Some of them dead. The smell of death. The woman let go of Camille's arm. Camille reached up to check her sensor and realized, for the first time, that she didn't have it in-game. She hoped that Robin was taking care of things. She smiled with some combination of relief and nerves.

"He's not to be trusted," Judith said as she dug her way out of the pile. "Camille, listen to me—"

The woman in red reached over and shoved Judith into the sea.

Camille watched as Judith sank. Her horror waned. She remembered again that this was a game. She knew that she would not die—would she?—but she was in danger: in danger of losing her practice, her office. In danger of losing the electricity required to keep her girlfriend charged. In danger of losing her own body. In danger of losing Robin altogether. Already they paid portions of bills in the hopes that the electric companies wouldn't shut them off completely.

"What exactly does this gameplay entail?" Camille asked, spread across the pile. "It's all over the place."

"It's the hackers," the man in the hat said. "How am I supposed to build a good game if we can't concentrate?"

The woman in the red dress leaned forward. "Have you figured out who they are?"

Camille looked from the man to the woman. "Which one are you, Mr. Moore?" They both laughed at the same time. "I'm both," the woman said. She winked.

Camille squirmed atop a naked body. He groaned as his blood soaked into Camille's clothes. "I was close," Camille said, "before you drowned that one in the ocean." She tried to scramble off the dying man, but bodies lay wherever she tried to plant her hands.

"I took some liberties to rescue you," the man in the hat said. "I'll be sending you to the next place where there's a vulnerability. Fix my game, Camille Maxwell. It's why I hired you."

"Any second now," Camille said. "I can't say I'm attached to this location."

The man rolled his eyes as the raft bumped onto the shore. He motioned at a yellow castle with a red roof that stood at the line where the ocean met the sand. The building had many windows. Camille stepped from raft to sand and left the nighthawks behind.

Inside the castle, the walls were lined with the posters of Mucha. Camille recognized the style, though she couldn't recall where she had seen them. The women on the posters were bright and beautiful and calming to look at. One sat in front of a ring of pink roses and wore flowers in her hair. Another wore a long blue dress and stood in front of a moon. Camille took several deep breaths. For the first time since she'd entered the game, she was at peace. One of the women had red hair and a red dress and winked as Camille walked past. Camille ignored her and continued. A ladder stretched up to the first of the four seasons: winter with her white robe, her white landscape.

Camille climbed the ladder then inside the poster. She shivered in the cold. The woman stood unmoving, staring out at something Camille could not see. For Camille, the world she had entered was, for the moment, three-dimensional, all-encompassing. Camille drew her name in the snow, and it morphed into the words: LES SAISONS. Camille waved to the woman even though the woman had not acknowledged her then walked on, toward other trees and a vast emptiness. She came to a place where the snow faded to grass, and white flowers sprouted before her eyes. In spring, the woman's long blonde hair blew around her ankles. She giggled once then froze, leaning forward with hands clasped near her shoulder. Summer was a thick redhead in a field of giant sunflowers. Camille appreciated her as she passed, but it was autumn who spoke: "Will you do me a favor and hold these for a sec?" The long-haired brunette handed Camille an armload of grapes.

She shook out her arms. "Thank fuck." She plucked several red flowers out of her hair. "I've been waiting a long time for you."

The season vibrated. Thin lines of static pulsed all around them.

"What now?" Camille said.

"Don't act like you're not starving," the woman said. "Though if you eat some of those grapes, you might just be stuck here."

"More mythology humor," Camille said. "Whoever you people are, I don't think you realize how much you have in common with the makers of this dumb game."

The woman massaged her arms. "Oh, we have a similar methodology, but different intentions." The woman held out her hand. "Harriet Hosmer," the woman said. "Or, the memory of her anyway."

"How many of you are there?" Camille said.

"I'm the same someone, really," Harriet said. "In many forms. We made backup plans, after all."

"What do you want?" Camille said. "What beef do you have with Mr. Moore?"

"Mr. Moore seems fine enough, innocuous even," Harriet said. "But this game. It could be such an opportunity, Camille Maxwell. I want to show you. Will you let me show you?"

Camille dropped the grapes onto the ground and took the woman's hand. "Yes, please. Clear it all up for me."

Harriet winked and tore off her wig to reveal short curls. She burst out of the autumn dress as a cicada may step out of its skin. Beneath it, she wore a tweed suit. "You like to dance?"

Camille did like to dance, though she had little time for it now. Robin had been built to enjoy it, to enjoy all forms of physical pleasure. No longer, Robin promised herself, and Camille had given up dancing to support her. But her body might be more versatile in a video game than in reality. Camille wondered what virtual reality might give her that she could not get elsewhere.

They fell through the floor and landed, this time, in a room made up of brushstrokes in shades of blue: the walls, the ceilings, the floor—all blue, a chaos of markings that did not, from up close, make a complete picture. Harriet laughed, her voice boisterous in the loud room, and Camille realized that several brushstrokes were moving, turning and leaping. In one direction, pink brushstrokes clapped, an audience. Camille squinted into the audience, and their hands formed the shapes of letters somehow: THE STAR. They were performing, Camille and Harriet and the other dancers.

"Pretend you're a good dancer," Harriet said. "For the sake of the game?"

Harriet turned and turned; she was indeed a good dancer, and clear amid the unsettled visions around her. Harriet stepped behind Camille, clasped two hands at her waist, and lifted Camille into the air. Camille formed an arc above her head with her hands. She laughed, and when Harriet tossed her into the air, she extended her legs in both directions before she stuck her landing. She met the floor with grace. She had never done ballet before, not even as a child, too unruly.

Camille heard in her head: *You're exerting a lot. Careful, Camille!*

But Camille wanted to keep dancing, and she ignored Robin until the music stopped, and she and Harriet took their bows to a roomful of applause. Camille's heart was racing, true, but as she sucked in lungfuls of deep breaths, she felt her body ache in the best of ways.

Harriet led Camille backstage, through the density of paint, through a door that Camille would not have been able to see. But no static greeted them as they walked.

"These parts of the game," Camille said. "Are they yours?"

Harriet shook her head. "We haven't done much here yet."

The door opened to a Paris street and a STARRY NIGHT sky, exaggerated swirls of deep blue and yellow and white, a beautiful crescent the color of egg yolk, a background of rolling blue hills. Harriet slid her arm in Camille's.

"I do love the impressionists," she said.

"Whose painting were you?" Camille said.

"My own," Harriet said. "I'm an artist."

"Are you trying to get to the end? Crash the party? Make your mark as a new artist, or something?"

Harriet laughed, and this laugh was not gentle but cruel. "I am not new. I was famous, in my day."

"Apologies," Camille said. She smelled the air; it smelled like a clear night. "What did you paint?"

"I'm a sculptor," Harriet said. "I sculpted women who were otherwise not given the treatment they deserved. Medusa, Daphne, Zenobia."

"I've never heard of Zenobia," Camille said.

"Of course not." Harriet stopped walking. "Famous Syrian queen. Why would you know anything about her?"

Harriet pointed toward a small café that looked closed. "There's a party in there," she said.

"How do you know?"

"I can sniff out a party from a hundred years away."

Harriet grabbed her hand. "Come!"

The cafe door opened into a field of pastels. Where before the brushstrokes had been long and graceful, now they were short and energetic, like the artist— THE MANY WORKS OF MATISSE, read a small sign on the backside of the door—had stabbed his brush again and again against the scenery. Trees with fat blue trunks and green leaves lined a stone walkway. The world was not homogenous; to either side of the path, people shaped like brightly colored kites moved about, fading in and out of static, the hackers' additions to Ashton Moore's Matisse kingdom.

"So, what's your purpose, Harriet?" Camille said. "You want to destroy the game?"

"Not at all!" Harriet bent to the grass and ran her hand along the strange paint splotches. "We want to use the architecture, the platform, that Mr. Moore has. It's proprietary, and he sues anyone who gets close to it, you know."

Camille did know; in their protest work, Robin and Camille made it their job to know what the rich men of the world were up to—and if there were ways to bring them down for it.

"Mr. Ashton Moore controls the virtual world. It may not seem like much, but believe me, it will be a world as populated as our own one of these days. We're only trying to build our own game, Ms. Maxwell. We're only trying to build something for everyone. For you. For me. For women. For misfits. For people who are not Mr. Ashton Moore."

"What would be the object of this game, then?"

"The finer details are yet to be discovered," Harriet said. "But we may leave some of the original game architecture."

A gust of wind traveled through the scene, and the kite people lifted into the air then dropped again. Camille and Harriet passed one of them; he wore a mirrored face.

"Picasso?" Camille guessed.

"Please," Harriet said. "We've given him the ax. These belong to Sonia Delaunay."

"I've never heard of her either," Camille said.

"But now you have!"

Harriet led Camille through the grass and over to a red-brown swath. As they approached, walls erected around them painted blue with patches of brown.

The red-brown swath was a floor, and cuts of black hair formed a trail through hallways. Camille followed Harriet until they reached a room with a chair in the middle. In that chair sat a woman in a suit holding a pair of scissors. Camille could not help herself; her stomach jumped at the sight of Frida Kahlo. There were no glitches in this room, and when Frida spoke, her voice a deep purr, it did not break.

"Hello there," she said. "Welcome to my room."

"And here—" Harriet said.

"I know Frida," Camille said, dropping her hand from Harriet's arm. "Don't insult me."

"A worldly woman you are!" Harriet said.

"My name is Frida Kahlo. I lived an interesting life. You're inside one of my portraits now. I come from Mexico. Where do you come from?"

"Uh." Camille frowned. "America."

"Bordering my beautiful country!" Frida said.

Camille looked at Harriet, who was staring intently back at Camille and grinning. "How interesting this all is!" she said.

"She's not as ... dynamic? As the other characters."

"Mr. Moore fails at writing women," Harriet said. "It's been a criticism of all of his games. I suppose you didn't research your generous benefactor."

"He pays," Camille said. "I can't afford to look into it."

"I married Diego Rivera in 1929. I loved him. He was a brilliant artist." Frida snipped off a final sprig of her hair.

Camille groaned. For the first time since she arrived, she wished she weren't there. "Can we move on?" she said.

"Not so fast." Harriet reached into her pocket and pulled out a small round disk.

"What's that?"

"Sentience." Harriet made her way over to Frida, who looked up from her chair but didn't move. "I have a treat for you."

Frida scowled. "Are you here to invite me to the party?" she said. "I love a good party."

"Open wide," Harriet said and placed her fingers on either side of Frida's mouth. Harriet shoved the disc through Frida's lips. Frida swallowed. Camille looked away, uncomfortable with the scene as it was playing out. But once the disc had passed down Frida's mouth, or whatever it had done, Frida belched.

"That was delicious," she said, and her eyes lit up as they landed on Harriet.

She stood, and the stray hairs in her lap fell around her, forming a grotesque flower. "I know you!" she said. "Or, I know of you. I was a baby when you died."

"I'm afraid so," Harriet said. "I would have given anything to meet you, Ms. Kahlo. Or to have known that you were coming to the art world."

"Ha! We are meeting now." Frida pulled Harriet's face toward hers and kissed her on both cheeks.

Harriet smirked. She gestured to Camille. Camille took a tentative step forward. "This is my friend," Harriet said.

"Is she an artist too?" Frida said.

"Not as such," Camille said. She stuck out her hand for Frida to shake.

"Come here, beauty." Frida held out her arms. Camille had no option but to hug the woman. She couldn't turn down a hug with Frida Kahlo, after all, and she should have no reason to beyond the strange discomfort that settled in her belly as she watched the two women stand in one another's company.

"I am covered in hair," Frida said. "I must change! We must have a drink! A dance!"

"I was thinking the same thing, Ms. Kahlo," Harriet said, extending her arm for Frida to latch onto. But Frida draped her arms around both women and led them through her empty rooms to the world outside: a brown landscape, flat and covered in giant broken-open rotting fruit and giant seashells. Frida stripped off her suit to reveal a red-and-white party dress, floor-length and rimmed with lace.

"Life isn't made for sitting in a room," she said. "It's made for this." She twirled around a bed of pomegranate ruins, flinging the seeds up with her feet as she moved. "Come here." She beckoned with one long finger toward Camille.

"You designed her well," Camille said.

"She's original to the game," Harriet said. "We just made her truer to her life."

Camille joined hands with Frida, and together they danced among the reek of rot. Camille laughed like she had not laughed in half a year.

Your levels are low, Robin said. *Your heart's beating fast. You're using up too much sugar. If you won't come out, then at least slow down.*

"You seem distracted, dear," Frida whispered into Camille's ear, and the whisper sent a shiver down her spine. Harriet held Camille's hand and spun her around. "We have so many places to show you!"

Please, I'm worried about you, Robin said.

"I can't," Camille said.

Frida frowned. Harriet's forehead wrinkled.

"I can't wait." Camille reached up and detached the wire that connected Robin's voice to hers. "Show me everything."

THE THREE WOMEN MADE THEIR way through a landscape of paint splatters and smears, pastel and bright. DE KOONING and POLLOCK weaved through the patterns.

"More men," Camille said.

"They're not!" Harriet said. Her eyes sparkled. "It's the work of their wives! We kept the names the same. They didn't even notice!"

They laughed together until they could not breathe, and then they lay on the dizzying floor until they could not tell one woman's limbs from another. Camille ran her hands along Frida's body, grabbing at the fat of her belly, kissing the space where her thigh met hip. The woman had known pain there. Harriet bid them lay side by side and teased them both with her fingers until they both came, a contest Frida won. Camille's body rocked, and as she rocked, she thought of Robin; would Robin know from the noises she made what she was up to? Would Robin care?

Once the women had gained back their breath, they chased one another through the abstract fields. Camille paused upon a triangle, and her body burned to remember how she had shut Robin out for worrying, for caring. Up ahead, Frida and Harriet raced along a sidewalk. Camille ran after. The floor opened up. She fell.

She landed in a white room. A trap. Harriet followed after.

"Minimalism?" Camille said, looking around.

A woman stepped out from the walls. Ashton Moore liked to step out of walls, Camille realized. First, the woman was white, then purple, then red. "Interrogation," Marilyn Monroe said.

Camille shielded her eyes from the single fluorescent bulb glaring above them. "This lighting."

"Dan Flavin," Harriet said. Camille realized, with a start, that Harriet's hands had been tied behind a Jacobsen egg chair while Camille had been allowed to stand free. Frida was nowhere to be found.

"I'm rescuing you," Marilyn said. "Though I'm also wondering why you, the most competent PI of this modern world, need to be rescued."

"I don't know where you've been reading your reviews," Camille said.

"Google," Marilyn said.

"Those can be inaccurate," Camille said.

"What exactly is going on here?" Marilyn said. She turned blue, then pink, then gold. "This should be finished by now. Who are these people? Who is she?" Marilyn gestured to Harriet.

"You don't know me?" Harriet said.

Frida broke free from her camouflage, her body the chair upon which Harriet had been strapped. She unfolded herself, a rose breaking open with the dawn. With Harriet stuck to her back, Frida lunged at Marilyn, her nails grown long in the moments between when Camille fell into the room and now. Frida held one long nail at Marilyn's throat. Marilyn turned red, then orange, then green.

Marilyn struggled beneath Frida's threat. "Camille, help me," she called out.

Camille looked from woman to woman; they could be anyone, outside their avatars. Frida was no one, just coding. Still, Camille would never forgive herself if she betrayed Frida Kahlo.

"Do what they say." Camille shrugged. "Or else."

MARILYN ESCORTED THEM, FRIDA'S SHARP nails poking her in her back, through the white walls to what the three women all referred to as the final level. On the other side of the white room, they climbed from one Murakami skull to the next, up a stairway of pop art. At the top of the stairs, they grabbed hold of a single red Banksy balloon. It lifted them through the dark air to an entrance guarded by a Haring dog with three heads.

"You've got to be kidding," Camille said.

"Just jump us there," Harriet said. "You're not fooling anyone."

Marilyn rolled her eyes, but she snapped her fingers, and as they flowed through the air, her skirt billowed out all around her. They landed in the middle of a blank room. A party formed around them. Men of all stripes mingled near a table full of snacks, on the dance floor, pressed against the walls like they didn't crave the attention. Camille frowned. She understood it all: how frustrating it must be, to love the possibility of what a game could be. To know you could make it better.

"You don't see anything wrong with this?" Camille said to Marilyn. "Nothing at all?"

"It's a room full of brilliant people," Marilyn said. "And—oh! Looks like Pollock's in the punch again."

Camille grabbed Marilyn by the shoulder before she had a chance to run. "They're all men," she said.

Marilyn studied the room. Her smile fell. "You're right." Then she laughed. "I hadn't noticed. How funny!" She gestured vaguely at Frida. "But what do you call her?"

"You made her dull as an old sculpting knife," Harriet said.

"But women are likely responsible for the bulk of cave art! Based on the model and measurements of the hands in our first level, 75 percent belong to women."

Harriet frowned. "Where in your game do you acknowledge that fact?"

"It's too late to change things now," Marilyn said. She smirked. "Camille, I assume you succeeded in your task here? Who are these jokers?"

Camille pursed her lips. "I don't know," she said.

"You seem cozy enough with them," Marilyn said. She turned pink, then green. "But there's a lot you don't know, isn't there, Camille?"

Camille squeezed Marilyn's shoulder tighter; it hit her, then, that she was no threat to Ashton Moore as Zeus, nor as the red-dressed woman from the diner, nor as Warhol's Marilyn. The hands with which she held onto him were not her real hands. The pressure she exerted upon him was virtual. She let go.

"I know about your girlfriend," Marilyn said, and she smiled an open mouth smile, and inside that smile were teeth made of 1's and 0's, and they spilled out as Camille's breath picked up, as she felt her head going light, as her vision became a pinprick of dark, and she fell.

"I'M ANGRY WITH YOU," ROBIN said as the glucose tablet melted under Camille's tongue. Camille stared up at their yellowed ceiling. "You understood that I would be angry with you. Yet you unplugged from me anyway."

"It's human behavior," Camille said. She reached her hands out and pulled Robin down to her. "I've been so stupid."

"Yes, it was stupid," Robin said. "I was supposed to be taking care of you."

"Please, take care of me," Camille said. Her mouth tasted sweet. She rolled over on the floor and kissed Robin's hand where it pressed the floor beside her. "I had a threesome with Frida Kahlo and Harriet Hosmer."

Robin laughed a single laugh. "You had a threesome with virtual characters."

"It felt so real."

"Sounds like a lovely game."

"It's not." Camille shook her head. "At least, not the one Ashton Moore wrote. Or the one the hackers hastily inserted. But together they've made this hodgepodge of buffoonery. Intrigue. I felt like I was in some cyberpunk detective story. I felt like my mind was in six places at once. It's been so long—" Camille stopped and brought her hands to her face. She curled into a ball. "Robin, he knows about you! Ashton Moore. Why do I keep trusting these goddamned billionaires?"

Robin held her hands against Camille's face. "Because you have no choice in the matter. They have all the money, Camille. Money that we need to do good. And, most importantly, to keep you healthy."

"If you're going to be rational about it." Camille's stomach throbbed with hunger, and likely some new stress-induced stomach issue she would have to ignore the doctor about. She was tired—of working for rich people, of hustling for jobs, of never knowing if she was ill or faking it, of feeling like she was faking it even when she was ill. Of convincing herself to fake improvement, so that she could live without constant worry, so that she could go one night without Robin needing to care for her. She needed Robin to care for her, Robin who could hold whole worlds inside her and not be overwhelmed by them. Camille sat up suddenly, and even though the act made her dizzy, she spoke with excitement. "I have an idea."

"I know what you're thinking." Robin grinned. "I want to play."

CAMILLE'S AVATAR WOKE UP WHERE she'd fallen: on the floor in the middle of the party. Marilyn tapped her foot as Camille's avatar opened her eyes. "Finally," Marilyn said. "Did you have a nice nap?"

"I had a lovely sleep," Robin said through Camille's virtual mouth. "Thank you for asking."

"Did you happen upon the names of these criminals while you were out?" Marilyn said.

Harriet rolled her eyes. "You've monopolized the whole industry. What else are we supposed to do?"

"Try working toward your goals instead of stealing what doesn't belong to you," Marilyn said.

"These worlds you've made are stolen," Robin said. She reached inside the game. It took a lot of processing power, but she could hack it, for the time being. She scanned the room. She grabbed Marilyn's mouth and opened it wide. She scanned the 1's and 0's inside, took all the code inside of her in an instant.

Marilyn shook her off and frowned. "What the hell, Camille?"

"You've changed the worlds, sure," Robin said, "but isn't that what Harriet here has done too?"

Frida danced around Camille's avatar. "Who are you?"

"She's been with us the whole time," Harriet said.

"I don't recognize her," Frida said.

"Harriet's got some good ideas too," Robin said. "Frida here? She learns as she interacts. She's mutable. Anyway, you've been fighting this whole time. But your games suck without one another. Ashton, you have the programming, but where's the excitement? And Harriet, your game glitches and lags. You can't have that going out to *consumers*."

"Your point?" Harriet said. She and Marilyn now stood side by side, staring Camille's avatar down.

Robin wandered over to the buffet table and poured herself a glass of merlot. She returned to the standoff, which had now become two-against-her-one.

"Once you work out terms together, I'll give you back your game," Camille said. "I'm expecting it to take no longer than three days. And it better include a fee for me. I'm thinking my original fee, plus extra for the consultation."

With that, Robin threw her wine into both of their faces and deleted the game in one fell swoop.

ROBIN FELL OUT OF THE game. Her battery indicator blinked red. Camille kneeled at her feet.

"I did it," Robin said. She laughed. "Here's hoping we don't get sued."

"I trust we can handle ourselves," Camille said. "And if our ransom goes well, we'll have enough to get by. And then some."

"What are we going to do for money until then?" Robin said. "I need to charge."

"I have credit cards." Camille winked. "And why don't you just upload more fake reviews of my services? Maybe a quick gig will pop up. Some cheating spouse. No billionaires required."

"I'm sure I don't know what you're talking about," Robin said. She removed a memory stick from her mouth and handed it to Camille.

Camille pocketed the stick. She wrapped her arms around Robin's legs. She knew that Robin could not feel her touch the way that Camille felt Robin's—but their bodies were warm, one from blood, the other from energy—and their lips sought each other's in the night—and they took care of each other—and they wouldn't let anyone, real or virtual, stand in their way.

ACKNOWLEDGEMENTS

FIRSTLY, I NEED TO THANK the editors who loved these stories enough to give them first homes: Meghan Bell at *Room*; Jason Henderson at Castle of Horror; Dash at Expanded Horizons; Christopher Evans at PRISM International; Andrew S. Fuller of Three-Lobed Burning Eye; Leah Bobet at Ideomancer; Andy Cox at *Interzone*; Sadye Teiser at *Masters Review*; Michael Damian Thomas and Lynne M. Thomas at Uncanny; and finally, Eric Bosarge and J M McDermott at Vernacular Press.

And for giving them second homes, in the form of reprints: Keffy R. M. Kehrli of Glittership; Steve Berman of Lethe Press; M. Benoît Domis at Ténèbres; Scott Silk at Tales to Terrify; Saurio at La Idea Fija; Mathew Garcia at Gaia; Michael Nye at Story; and Jeremy Szal at StarShipSofa.

Thanks to my agent, Hannah Bowman.

I wouldn't be the writer I am today without my family: my parents, Jenny and Eddie; my sister, Rachel; my nephews, Silas and Ian; my brothers-in-law, Tommy and Andrew; and my parents-in-law, Carolyn and Bob.

Thanks, also, for Ellie Alonzo, for the brilliant cover photography.

And thank you to William, whose undying support sustains me every day.

BONNIE JO STUFFLEBEAM is the author of the horror novel *Grim Root*, the short story collection *Where You Linger & Other Stories*, and the horror novella *Glorious Fiends*. Her short fiction and poetry have appeared in over 90 publications, such as *Popular Science*, *Lightspeed*, and *Le Var Burton Reads*, as well as in six languages. By night, she's a two-time finalist for the Nebula Award. By day, she works as a Narrative Designer writing games for a mobile app. She lives in Texas with her partner and a mysterious number of cats.

ABOUT THE AUTHOR

Printed in the USA
CPSIA information can be obtained
at www.ICGtesting.com
LVHW040531010424
776045LV00004B/309